RISE

CAITLYN E. GILMORE

authorHOUSE®

AuthorHouse™
1663 Liberty Drive
Bloomington, IN 47403
www.authorhouse.com
Phone: 1 (800) 839-8640

Published by AuthorHouse 09/18/2019

ISBN: 978-1-7283-2574-3 (sc)
ISBN: 978-1-7283-2575-0 (e)

Library of Congress Control Number: 2019913089

Print information available on the last page.

This book is printed on acid-free paper.

Dedicated to my loving family and friends

PROLOGUE

The Third War came at a time when everything was some sort of movement. Every song had political undertones. Art was a representation of stepping out of the box's society set, and dance was a revolt. The arts were a way for the younger generation to speak up and speak out against the injustices they felt were being done.

The war was a long time coming. Leaders all over the world were butting heads over everything. Threats were made countless times from every corner. Somehow, the country that once rested here was always in the middle of it. Even its allies were getting sick of having its back. When the war began, everyone thought it was the end of the world. Maybe, in a way, it was.

After all resources were gone and the war came to a halt, there was nothing for any country to rebuild from. At least not to what it once was. This country split into territories, each with a different kind of government. This story begins in a territory run by cruel, unfair, murderous leaders. They use fear as a form of control. They also got rid of whatever was left of art, literature, and music. There are pictures hanging in the council headquarters' lobby of a giant fire. You can make out titles of Old-World books and songs. Painted canvases melt in the flames. No one thought anything of it.

With creativity gone, our council recreated schooling. Most normal subjects were tossed aside. We still have history. Mathematics and sciences were shaved down and are now the same class. But instead of gym class, we have hand-to-hand combat. Instead of literature, weapons class. School is less school and more "How to Create a Solider 101." You go six days a week for about ten hours. There are no more sports teams or school dances. No extracurriculars. When you graduate from the academy, you have two choices. Go to work for the New World Order as a solider or someone in government. Or you become a commoner, working in shops, restaurants, and the like. Commoners are looked down on by anyone working for the New World Order. They are seen as weak.

When I graduated, almost two years ago now, I became a soldier. I never wanted to be a target. Commoners are always targeted. My older sister became a commoner, and our father hates her for it. He works with the council. When our mother was alive, she worked for the council but hated it. She hated herself for it, but sometimes we do things just to survive. It's all I've been doing my entire life.

I made sure I was good at what I do. I moved up through the ranks fast because I worked hard. I never wanted to be questioned by the people in power. When they question you, you're put on a list, and it's only a matter of time before you're executed. Everything I have done, it's all been survival. I've been called many names these past few months: traitor, bastard, and even the devil himself. I've hurt many people, including people I have come to care about.

If you're reading this, it means there is hope. It means everything I have done has been worth it. Don't get the wrong idea; it wasn't just me. Frankly, this was all because of *her.* If we die for this, I want to know it was worth something. For you to understand anything I am saying, I have to take you to the beginning of what many call the Rising.

CHAPTER 1

The chapel bells ring, singing their songs for the whole town to hear, followed by a solitary pitch ringing eight times. My father stirs in the room beside me, and I can only assume my sister, Sonia, is already gone for the day. I take one look at myself in the mirror. My uniform is all black. There is a patch with my last name on it and on the other side, my number. I leave the room as my father leaves his. His suit is crisp and clean. He stops and looks back at me.

"What zone are you in today?" he asks casually as I walk past him to the kitchen. He follows.

"North zone," I answer and grab a granola bar from the counter. North zone is where his office is. He always tries to normalize our relationship by offering to meet up for lunch. It never works.

"We should get lunch," he smiles.

I only glance at him.

"Yeah, you know, it's just a packed zone, and there's really no time for a break when I'm there," I tell him.

He sighs and nods.

"Right. Well then, have a productive day, son," he says flatly and grabs his keys, leaving abruptly and being sure to slam the door. *Productive. Not good. Productive.*

"You too," I mutter.

I get in my car and make my way to headquarters. The woman at the front desk signs me in for the day, which tells my bosses that I showed up, and then she hands me my assignment folder. That tells me what my tasks are for the day. Before I can leave, I am greeted by my commander.

"Ozera," he barks.

I nod at him. "Sir."

"My office. Now," he orders. Without question or hesitation, I turn on my heel and follow him to his office. He closes the door behind us and sits at his desk. I stand with my hands and folder behind my back. "Sit down, soldier." I do as I am told. "You're a good solider, Ozera. You really are. I want you to know that you've worked your ass off to be one of the best."

"Thank you, sir."

"Shut up," he waves his hand at me. "Have you opened your folder yet, boy?"

My commander is an older gentleman from what was once a state called Texas. Down there, everyone had a gun, an interesting accent, and an attitude. That's where he grew up.

"No, sir, not yet," I tell him. He motions toward the black folder in my hand and proceeds to lean back in his chair and chew his thumbnail.

I open the folder and begin to read. It only states one task. I have to find and observe a girl named Wren Adler. She is nineteen and suspected of having close ties to a possible resistance. There are three candid photos of her around North zone. She's small, weak looking. Her pale face is the definition of innocence and purity. I glance up at my commander.

"Commander Jackson," I begin. But then I turn the page and continue to read her description. She is the youngest of four. She has three older brothers; all of them are commoners. Her mother is on the council, and her father is a commander for Unit 8 of the New World Order Army. Wren is currently a model student at the academy. The only blemish on her record is that she got into a physical altercation with a male student one year above her earlier this year. It does not say why.

"Do you understand your mission?" he asks.

"Mission? This is a long-term order?"

"Today your task is as stated. But you've been chosen to play a key role in the mission of finding the resistance."

"Why me and why her? What makes you think she has anything to do with it?"

"Her father suspects she is involved. She vanishes every day from after academy lets out, to midnight," he turns to his computer and starts typing. "Don't let this next part go to your head, Maksim," he says with a smile. "But you're the best-looking soldier who isn't a knucklehead," he chuckles. *Excuse me?*

"What does that have to do with the mission?" I ask. He groans and looks at me with an amused expression, which is very different from his normal brick-face.

"She's a young pretty girl. You're not much older than her. You can get close to her." Now it all clicks. "First things first. Get out of that uniform. You're a commoner now, as far as she needs to know. You work for your sister in the bakery. I've already sent notifications to your father and Sonia, making them aware of this mission. They know the drill if you ever bring Wren around them."

"Sir, how close to I have to get to her?" I snap.

"As close as it takes. If you have to marry her to find out, you better do it," he snaps back.

"This could all be a very big waste of tim," I shake my head and stand.

"Then it's your time wasted for the good of the NWO." he shrugs. "Go on now. Get changed and get huntin'," he orders.

I go home, change into normal clothes, and then head to North zone. I leave my car in a lot close to the academy and make my way to the big brick building where I spent fourteen years of my life. I walk into the office and see a familiar face. She smiles up at me from her desk and shakes her head. I'm sure my commander informed the staff of the academy that I would be coming.

"Boy, when I heard you would be stopping back here, I got all kinds of giddy," the secretary beams and stands.

"How have you been, Bethany?"

"Wasting away here at this desk," she shakes her head. "But you! Almost two years out of the academy, and now you're a soldier. Amazing!"

"Yeah," I lower my voice. "So I assume you know why I am here." She nods. "We all do."

"I need some information on this girl. I need to know who I am dealing with," she nods again, very dramatically, and motions me to follow her.

I walk around her desk and follow her into the very back office, which is used as a file room now. She opens one of the drawers and fingers through the folders. She pulls out a big one with Wren's name on it.

Before handing it over, she locks the drawer and looks around. "This is everything we have about her from the time she started at the academy," she says.

"Thank you very much. You're doing a great service to the New World Order," I tell her, knowing it would make her feel good as well as shut her up.

She smiles and pats my cheek.

"Let me know if you need anything else," she says and leaves, closing the door behind her.

I sit at the desk in the far corner and open the folder. I read through every grade she has ever gotten, every report done on her. It takes hours, but I won't let anything slip through the cracks. She is a perfect student. When I get to earlier this year, I see the disciplinary report. I hold it up and begin to read. The report was written by the Head Administrator of the Academy. It says,

"Wren Adler was found beating fellow student Jeremy Hayes in the West Wing on October 5, 2088. Jeremy was on the floor with a broken nose, fractured wrist and bruises on his ribcage. Wren had a significant bruise on the left side of her face and bruises on her arms. When Administrators were finally able to pry Ms. Adler away from Mr. Hayes, she admitted to starting the altercation with Mr. Hayes but insisted it was an act of self-defense.

Upon further investigation we found that there was a history between the two students, and it was drawn to our attention by an outside source that the relationship was abusive. Ms. Adler apologized to us for her actions but refused to speak with or even go near Mr. Hayes. Both students were disciplined for their actions and it was made known that the incident would go on their permanent records.

Ms. Alder and Mr. Hayes have had no contact with each other inside or outside of this Institution and it is expected to stay that way until both have graduated. Ms. Adler has not displayed any other behavior of violence or poor attitude. She continues to excel in all areas of study."

~ Anthony Martz

I close the folder as the buzzer sounds for the next class to begin. I emerge from the office and take the folder to Bethany at the front desk. After thanking her again, I go to the gymnasium where Wren has self-defense class.

Teachers see me and smile but know not to engage. I wait along the far wall as students come out of the locker rooms in their sweatpants and tee shirts. I spot Wren Adler coming out with two other girls. Her fawn colored hair is pulled back into a knot on top of her head. Various strands have fallen out and frame her small, pale face. Her sweatpants are too long so she rolled them up and her tee shirt hangs on her. Her friends are taller than her. Mostly everyone is. She doesn't say much but laughs when the others do. She looks like a normal girl to me.

She can definitely fight. That becomes clear throughout the class. Her petite stature plays in her favor during fighting. She is a smaller target and she's fast. She's not perfect though. Her opponents get a few good hits in too. One guy takes her down … hard. She gets back up but is wobbly and looks even paler than before. The instructor calls them to stop and dismisses the class. That was her last class of the day, so I wait outside the academy for her to come out.

When she does, her hair is down instead of in the knot and she isn't with friends or smiling. I glance at my watch. 6:45. She turns down an alley. I begin to follow from a distance. After several turns and alley's, it's clear she's headed out of town. After a sudden turn, I lose her. I swear under my breath and look around for any sign of her. We are on the edge of town. there is nothing but ruin beyond here.

"Hey," a sharp voice hisses from above me. I look up and see her sitting on a stack of concrete slabs beside me. I don't reply. "Is there a reason why you're following me?" she demands. I force myself to laugh.

"Following you? Maybe you were following me," I reply.

She crosses her arms and looks out at the rubble. "Right, and that's why I am up here, and you are down there looking lost."

"Maybe I was just concerned about a little girl like yourself coming out here all alone. It's dangerous you know. Criminals hide out in these parts," I tell her.

She glares down at me.

"Little girl? Get lost," she snaps.

"Wow, okay. Let's try again," I step closer to the stack of slabs.

"I said get lost, stalker," she grumbles.

"Hey, I wasn't stalking," I counter. My mind scrambles for what to say next. "Maybe I just wanted to meet you. I saw you in the Academy. You were uhm … pretty amazing in there," I clear my throat and shift my weight from foot to foot.

"Yeah? Well I'm wondering what you were doing in the Academy, considering you graduated two years ago," she scoffs.

"I was delivering for my sister. She owns a bakery. I thought I would stop in since I was close and check things out," I lie.

"Why would a Commoner want to come back to that dump?" she asks.

"Well … I just had a feeling I should be there when I was," I do my best to keep my composure.

Her eyes narrow and she clenches her jaw, irritated.

"You're really bad at this," she grumbles.

"Bad at what?" I ask.

"Lying," she raises her eyebrows. "Are you going to tell me why you actually followed me out here?" she questions. I don't answer. She looks out at the rubble again.

"Why are you here?" I move closer to the tower.

She pats the empty space beside her.

"Come look," she says. I hesitate for a moment, but then climb the stack and sit beside her. From up here, I can see over the rubble and the sun which is setting. The horizon is painted with oranges, pinks, reds, purples. All blending together. It makes the sky look warm, despite the air.

"I see," I mutter.

"Just a moment or two of peace," she shrugs. The breeze blows her hair away from her face and neck. She has very light freckles on her cheeks and nose. Her eyes are a very light brown. There's a little scar, right beside her left eye. I wonder if that Jeremy kid did that to her.

"I'm Maksim. Maksim Ozera," I hold out my hand to her. She looks at it and then at my face. She shakes my hand and smiles slightly. "I know the Academy trains everyone to be skeptical of everyone, but you don't need to be so cold miss –"

"Wren Adler," she tells me.

"Do you really come out here just for the sunset?" I ask after a long silence.

She answers, "Partially."

"Tell me about yourself, Wren Adler," I sigh.

She draws her eyebrows together.

"Is this an interrogation?" she looks over at me.

"Guilty conscience?" I raise my eyebrow at her. Her cheeks flush and she looks away.

"No. I just don't know you," she tells me.

"Well that's how this works. You get to know someone by telling them about yourself and they do the same. It's how friendship works," I smile.

She laughs and shakes her head. "Why don't you start. Tell me about you," she says and looks at me again.

"Well … there isn't much to tell. My father is on the Council. My sister owns a bakery and I work for her," I tell her.

"That tells me nothing about you," she mumbles.

"What do you want to know?"

"Why did you choose to be a Commoner?" she questions.

"I uh … I can't kill the way they do. I can't be the reason for broken families. They expect everyone to be their puppets. I'm not about that," I answer.

I look down at my boots and clench my jaw. I do what I have to, to survive. I do what I have to, to give myself and my family a comfortable life. It's hard enough with Sonia being a Commoner. Two of us in the same family … we would be asking for mistreatment or worse … death.

I'm in control of my own life. This mission is for the good of all of us. If there is a resistance group, they could destroy everything the N.W.O has worked to create. I am just playing a role. This isn't real. I can't let it be personal.

"That's how I feel," she breathes and closes her eyes as the wind blows harder. "They don't own me. They don't own any of us. They think they do. Fools," she chuckles to herself.

"Your turn," I mumble.

She opens her eyes.

"My dad is a Commander in the Army. He's gone a lot. My mom is on the Council. They are both miserable. Mom is miserable because of dad. My older brothers are Commoners for the same reason you are. We don't want to give up our lives for them," her voice is thick with disgust.

"You do really well in the Academy for someone who doesn't want to help them," I nudge her. She glances down at my elbow and back up at my eyes.

"That's the ironic part. They train us to fight like them and be like them. They don't even consider the possibility of us using the skills they teach us to fight back," she whispers.

"Fight back?" I force myself to breathe evenly and not let my voice get too rigid. If she's going to spill to me right now, she's not as smart as I anticipated.

She shrugs and smiles.

"But what do I know? I plan on being an artist ... maybe bring back some creativity in this world. Mind my own business and hope they don't come to kill me for God knows what reason," she tells me.

I swallow the lump in my throat.

"Yeah ..." I croak.

The sun is setting faster. The oranges and reds are swallowed by the dark purples. The early December wind picks up.

"I should be getting home," she says and starts to climb down to the ground.

Home? What is going on? It's only sunset.

"I'll walk you," I say as I reach the ground.

She scoffs at me.

"I can handle myself."

"If you don't let me, I'll just have to follow you again," I shrug and look down at her.

She rolls her eyes and tucks her hands in her coat pockets.

"Fine," she agrees.

We walk back through the alley's and reach the main street. It's not busy, but there is life besides us. Several guards pass me, knowing not to address me. I feel their eyes. We are walking towards the gated community where high-ranking officials of the Council live.

"What exactly does your mom do on the Council?" I ask her.

"Vice President," she answers. I feel like I was punched in the gut. What child of a Vice President is going to join a resistance?

"Wow ..." I mumble. We reach the gate. She scans her ID and it opens.

"You don't have to come if you want to get home. It's cold out and it's getting colder," she says softly. It's dark now. Her eyes repel the darkness around us and somehow illuminate her face.

"I want to see you again," I blurt out. She looks surprised.

"No ... you don't," she smiles and backs away from me. She closes the gate, putting metal bars between us.

"I'll just follow you again," I tell her.

"You'll have to find me first," she smirks and walks away.

I catch myself smiling. I clear my throat and turn away from her, heading back towards town. As I get to my car, I get a call from my Commander telling me to meet him at a diner in East Zone. It takes me less than ten minutes to get there. I see him sitting in a booth in a corner. It's odd to see him in something other than his uniform. He has a big folder sitting in front of him with a cup of coffee.

I enter the diner and make my way towards him. His eyes don't move from their fixation on the coffee cup. He looks older when he isn't in his uniform. More like an old grandpa rather than a Commander in the biggest, toughest Army in the world. It's amazing how that works. With the uniform, we are intimidating, powerful soldiers. Without it ... he's old and weak. And I'm just some guy ...

Maybe that's part of the New World Order illusion.

"Sit down," he says gruffly. I do as I am told. He holds his coffee cup in his hands and stares me down. There is nothing old man-like about him now. He could beat my ass to a bloody pulp at any second and no one would dare try to stop him.

"Sir?"

"Commander Adler contacted me tonight. He said his daughter came home right after the sunset around 7:30," he tells me.

"Yes. I walked her back to the gated community after the sun was down. She didn't seem to have any intentions of going anywhere else," I reply.

"She's a smart girl. She wouldn't just suggest you come with her. Tell me everything. Did you build a level of trust?" he asks.

I proceed to tell him everything that I read about her, saw from her and everything that happened once she found me. I leave out anything I think personally of her. I agree she's smart. There's a lot going on in that head of hers. I can see it in her eyes. I noticed her eyes a lot …

They aren't just brown, but they have flecks of gold in them. And her light freckles on her cheeks and nose. I didn't mention the little scar beside her left eye or how long her eyelashes were.

It's not relevant what I notice about her appearance. Only her actions are important. When I finish telling him how I walked her to the gate and about the flirtatious interaction that occurred before coming here, he starts laughing and clapping. I look around, embarrassed.

"I knew you were the guy for the job! You have … what do the kids call it? Game? Is that right?" he cackles.

"I'm just trying to get the information we need," I grumble, suddenly irritated.

"You're doing a damn decent job! What's your next move?" he leans forward like a schoolgirl listening to gossip.

I roll my eyes and shove my hands in my jacket pockets.

"It would be odd to see her tomorrow. I'm going to have to watch her from a distance. It's going to be hard to follow her to the outskirts without her noticing. You can see everything from the concrete slab tower. I'm going to have to figure something else out," I think aloud.

"Track her," he shrugs, taking a sip of black coffee.

"How am I supposed to do that?" I snap.

He leans back and groans.

"Request access to her cell phone tracking chip from the Mobile Security Unit and have them set it up on your phone. The office opens at 8 tomorrow morning," he answers. I nod and clear my throat.

"Is that everything? I should be going," I tell him. He nods and we both stand. In the parking lot, he grabs my arm.

"One last thing," he says. I look at him. "I meant what I said," he pauses. "I knew you were the guy for the job," he smiles. I smile back and nod.

The drive back to my house in West Zone is long and quiet. I never play the radio. It's just propaganda anyway. I get home and before I can get to my room, my sister calls my name from hers.

"Maksim Ozera, you idiot!" she yells as I enter the doorway. In her fist is the letter my Commander probably sent to her. Her eyes are dark with fury and general irritation. "What are you doing, playing spy?! For *them*!" she snaps.

"*Them*?" I hiss. "I chose to work for *them* because there is nothing wrong with what we do! I *am* one of *them*!" I yell back. She stands up from her bed. She may be three years older than me, but I tower her by a couple inches.

"You always say that and sometimes I wonder who you are trying to convince. Me … or yourself," she growls.

"I am doing what is right for the greater good. A resistance is the last thing this country needs," I feel my face flushing with anger.

"A resistance is *exactly* what this country needs!" she screams. I feel something inside me snap. I try to leave and slam her door, but she catches it and throws it back open. I turn on my heel and head towards my room. "Don't stomp away from me when you know I am right!" she pesters.

I turn on her.

"What do *you* know about the resistance? Hm? Because right now you are looking awfully guilty of being involved, Sonia," I mutter through clenched teeth.

She laughs.

"Even if I wanted to be a part of that, I could never get around you and dad. It's like I am a prisoner in my own house!" she shoves me. Before I can react, I see dad behind her.

"You are welcome to leave anytime," he says calmly.

Sonia looks back at him.

"I plan on it," she grumbles, shooting me one last glare before storming off to her room. I look at my father and take a deep breath to calm myself down.

"She may be bitter … but she is no revolutionary," he smiles lightly. I nod in agreement. "This is a huge honor, son. To be chosen for this," he moves closer. "What's the girl like?" he asks. I swallow and glance away from him briefly. When I look back at him, his eyebrows are raised. *Impatient bastard.*

"She's perfect," I answer and mentally kick myself. "As student I mean. She is a star student and a model citizen," I look down at my boots.

"Not what I imagine when I think of a rebel," he shrugs. I nod again. "Well ... if there is something to find out ... you will find it, Maksim," he pats my shoulder and starts to walk away.

"Her mom is the Vice President of the Council," I blurt out. He stops and looks back at me.

"Elissa Adler's daughter?" he gasps.

"Wren," I tell him. He laughs a little and rubs his jawline. "Her father is the one that reported her suspicious behavior. Don't mention it to your fellow Council members. I'm not sure if her mother even knows," I tell him. He smiles and nods. I turn and go to my room, closing the door as fast as I can.

I fall back on my bed and groan internally. She's too smart to catch easily and I'm too bad at being what I need to be to get close to her. It's going to take maximum effort. My sleep is interrupted frequently. Sonia's words race around my head. She has no idea what she is saying. She's just bitter. That's all there can be to it. She never stopped grieving after mom died. She's taking out her pain on the easiest target ... that's all. She's wrong.

CHAPTER 2

The following days are filled with nothing but me spying on Wren. It becomes boring if I'm being honest. I don't get close enough for her to spot me at any moment. I track her phone. Every morning she goes for a run in the gated community at 7, goes home, I assume she showers and then is at the Academy by 8:30. After that, she goes back to the outskirts and stays there until midnight. She doesn't move. It's almost odd. Maybe she's just a creature of habit.

After about a week of only tracking her, I decide that it's time to approach again. I think hard about some of the things she might say about me being gone or questions she might ask about the article I claim to have been writing. I plan everything to a T in my head. She's not going to trip me up. She may be smart, but I'm smarter.

The Academy bell rings and students pour out of the door. I lean against my car which is parked right in front of the Academy steps. I watch for her carefully with my arms crossed and face blank. No one pays mind to me. I hear laughter before seeing her come out with her two friends again. They all start to walk down the stone steps until she stops. Her eyes meet mine and her milky white cheeks turn pink. Her friends look back at her and then follow her gaze to me. They giggle and whisper. She shushes them and makes her way down the steps to me.

Why does my chest feel tingly? What is that? It needs to stop. I need to stop.

"Hey stranger," she says in a cold voice. Her friends watch closely and continue to giggle.

"Ouch. Missed me that much?" I push myself away from the car. I tower over her and I can tell she doesn't like it. She steps back a little.

"I don't like when people waste my time," she growls.

"Waste your time? How have I wasted your time if I haven't even been around, Wren?" I ask with a light tone.

"You can't just show up and act … I don't know … interested … and then vanish for a week," she rambles. I see her bite the inside of her cheek and she hugs herself to stop from fidgeting. I put my hands up calmly.

"I've been around. I've just been letting you live your life. Would you rather I make it known when I'm stalking you?" I ask playfully. I watch her face relax and a glimmer returns to her eyes.

"Please. I would know if you were stalking me," she purrs.

That's where you're wrong.

"Hm. Right well … I don't want to waste your time, so I'll be going. I was going to ask you to get dinner, but you have company," I glance up at her friends before turning away from her.

"Dinner?" she scoffs. I face her again. She clears her throat. "Like … together?"

Her friends whisper and giggle more.

"Yeah, you know, like … I open the car door for you and take you somewhere tacky and cheap and we talk and then I walk you to your door and your dad gets mad that we were out so late and –"

"I don't think that kind of stuff happens in real life," she cuts me off. *It used to.* She chews the inside of her cheek some more. It must be a nervous tick.

"Is that a yes or no?" I sigh. She looks back at her friends. They nod dramatically and walk away from her, giggling still. Completely obnoxious.

She looks back at me, eyes narrowed.

"Are you going to murder me if I get in the car with you?" she asks.

"I don't think that kind of stuff happens in real life," I repeat her words. She laughs and tucks a strand of hair behind her ear.

"Okay, fine. I'll go with you," she agrees. I feel my heart skip. I don't like it. "But I get my own car door, okay?" she points at me.

"Get in," I smile and open my own door. She walks around the front of the car and gets in the passenger seat.

I start heading towards the diner in East Zone where I met my Commander the other night. Wren watches me carefully for the first minute we are in the car. After a long silence, she reaches up and turns on the radio. I look over at her as she finds a station she likes. It's actual music. I didn't know there was any stations with actual music.

"Don't you listen to music?" she asks. I shake my head no. "Why not?" she questions.

"I don't know. I like the quiet." I shrug and smile at her. She presses her lips together and looks forward, nodding along with the song.

The rest of the car ride is without conversation. When we pull into the parking lot, her eyes light up. She looks over at me, smiling. I turn off the car and open my door. She doesn't move.

"What?" I ask.

"I love this place," she answers.

This place is garbage. She could afford to go anywhere.

"Well, let's go then," I get out of the car. She leaves her backpack in my front seat and practically skips to the door.

She opens the door and stands back, motioning for me to go before her. I sigh and reach above her, opening the door more myself. She glares and goes ahead of me. When we get inside, she greets the waiter by name. His smile reaches ear to ear as he comes around the counter to greet her. They hug and then he looks at me.

Maybe he's why she loves this place.

"Who's this?" he asks.

"This is my new friend Maksim," she nudges my arm with her elbow and smiles back at the waiter. It's not a smile I've seen from her before.

"Well he must know you pretty well to know to bring you here! Go ahead to your booth, sweetheart. I'll be with you in a minute," he smiles and disappears into the back.

As we sit down in the two-person booth in the corner, I put my hands in my pockets, unsure of what to say. What's up with that guy? He's gotta be a little older than me. Why's he so interested in her?

"You good?" her voice brings me back from my own head.

"I'm great." I shrug.

The waiter; Peter; brings us two menus.

"What'll it be to drink?" he asks me.

"Just water," I grumble.

"And I assume your regular?" he smiles at Wren. She nods, and he leaves again.

"You have a regular?" I ask her.

"Hot green tea with a teaspoon of honey." she tells me. I nod and look out the window at nothing. "What's up with you?" she asks.

"What's up with him?" It slips out. I mentally kick myself almost a hundred times for how upset I let myself sound.

"Whoa," she chuckles. "He's been a good friend for a long time. Knows my brother's well."

"Just a friend? You sure about that?" I force myself to keep my tone light.

It's not like I actually care or anything ... I just don't want anyone getting in the way of me getting my information. That's all ...

"Of course," she smiles and shakes her head.

"Does he know that?" I whisper.

She laughs more and crosses her arms.

"I guess it doesn't matter what he thinks. What does any of this matter?" she demands.

"Hey, I just want to make sure I'm not hanging around someone else's girl," I tell her.

She raises her eyebrows at me. Her smile fades away.

"Someone's girl? Look, I'm not anyone's anything. I don't belong to anyone. Even if I was with him, I wouldn't be his to have. No one can own me." she snaps, pointing at me angrily. I can't stop myself from smiling.

I lean forward and look her in the eye.

"Good to know," I shrug and stare her down until her face softens.

"Great," she mutters and lets her hands slide down to her lap. Peter comes back and takes our order. She gets pancakes and I get a chicken sandwich. After Peeping Peter leaves, I turn my attention back to Wren.

"It's nighttime," I state.

"So? Pancakes are better at night," She smiles and sips her tea.

I shake my head. "Odd." "I wish I knew enough about you to be judgy," she counters. "What's your family like?"

"I told you before."

"No," she rolls her eyes. "You told me what they do. You didn't tell me what they are like or anything," she leans forward. Our faces are closer now.

"What do you want me to say? My father is a major ass and my sister … well … she's a lot like you," I tell her. "She values her independence and doesn't settle," I add. She smiles.

"What about your mom?" she rests her head on her hands.

I look down.

"She died a few years ago. Sickness," I tell her.

"I'm so sorry," she whimpers.

"Hey, don't be. A lot of people died from that illness. I mourned and moved on," I shrug.

Except Sonia and I weren't allowed to see her once she got sick. Only our father could see her. When she was buried, it was a closed casket and a small ceremony. There was no saying goodbye.

The rest of dinner is spent eating talking about lighter topics. She tells me about her brothers and her parents. She talks about how she was raised. Her parents never agreed on parenting styles. Her mother was always about independence and being your own person, but her father thought she needed to conform to societies idea of a perfect citizen. Wren says she tries her best to be both.

The car ride to the community is quiet, besides the radio. When we get to the gate, I turn off the car and look over at her. She is looking down at her hands and fiddling with a ring she wears on her left index finger.

"Thank you for joining me," I murmur. She smiles over at me.

"Thanks for inviting me. I had fun, actually. I didn't think I would. I did though," she says.

"Yeah me too," I smile down at the steering wheel. It's actually the truth. "You're not the kind of person I thought you were," I mutter. *Shut up, shut up.*

"I could say the same about you," she replies. I look over at her. "Are you going to vanish for another week?" she asks playfully.

"Do you want me to?" I counter. She shakes her head no.

We sit there in silence for a long time. Her face is so close. I catch myself as I glance at her lips and she catches it too. The corner of her mouth pulls up just a little. I look away again and swallow the growing lump in my throat. She sighs and reaches for the door handle.

Her voice is barely audible as she says, "Night, Mak." Goosebumps cover my skin. *Mak?*

"Night," I croak.

I watch her vanish past the gates and then let myself slam on the steering wheel. I'm losing my mind. She is just a job. She is an assignment. She is probably the enemy. I cannot let myself get emotionally involved for real. I can't let her play me either. For all I know, she knows what I'm really doing. She could be playing me as much as I am playing her. I am playing her. That's how this works. I can't feel bad about it.

We have a few "dates" to follow over the weeks. Commander Jackson calls me for another in person update. I go to his office and sit down, waiting. He comes in and sits in his chair. He fiddles with his paperwork and then finally looks up at me.

"How's the mission? Have any information yet?" he asks.

"Sir, I believe I have gotten fairly close to Wren. There is no sign of her being a resistance member. We've been together a lot and when we aren't, she is in the Academy or watching the sunset outside of town. I don't think she has to be a suspect anymore," I tell him. His eyes narrow. I sit quietly and wait for him to say something.

"How close?" he asks.

"Sir?"

"How close have you gotten?" he clarifies.

"I'm ... I don't know. Close enough, I guess. She trusts me. She would have mentioned it by now ... I think," I stumble.

"Do you think she's smart?"

"Very, Sir," I nod.

"Have you come to care for her?" he growls. I don't answer. "Answer me, Soldier."

"Yes, Sir. I have," I sigh. He leans back in his seat and crosses his arms.

"And you enjoy spending time with her?"

"Commander Jackson, I would not feel any way about her if there were cause for concern. I am doing my job," I hiss.

He scoffs at me.

"You better be. Get me answers. I know that rat is up to something. Figure it out. Don't let your pathetic emotions get in the way of what is important. Don't make me regret assigning you this mission," he warns. "Now get out of my office."

I stand up and start to leave.

"Maksim," he calls. I look back at him.

"The only reason she trusts you is because she doesn't know who you really are," he tells me. I leave his office, fuming. *Get your head clear and get focused.*

One Sunday before church service, everyone is filling into the chapel. I spot Wren with her family. Her three brothers surround her. The oldest one banters with Wren and the other two keep quiet, watching her father carefully. He looks like a harsh man. I've spoken to him once before, months before this mission. He wasn't polite to say the least.

My father, Sonia and I go to our usual seats, which are across the aisle and two rows back from Wren's family. I watch her carefully throughout the service. During the hymn's she sings, without needing to look in the book and during the message, she is into it. She'll occasionally nod and mumble "amen" with other's around the pews. Afterwards, she meets my eyes and her cheeks get pink. I turn my attention to Sonia for the walk out to the grass, where everyone hangs out for a while to talk. While my father talks to fellow Council members and Sonia chats with some girls she knows, I watch Wren.

She only interacts with her brothers and Peter when he comes over. He seems more friendly with her older brother. They must be good friends. Our eyes occasionally meet, but she will quickly look away. Out of the corner of my eye, I see four Soldiers march into the grass from across the street with President Zurek behind them. They shove through the crowd and grab a man from his family. He is a commoner. They drag him out into the open and force him to his knees.

While two hold him, the other two point their guns at him. A hush falls over the crowd. Wren looks horrified and her brothers look like they could kill. Her mother stands with her arms crossed and a blank expression but her father ... he smiles.

"Pardon the intrusion on this beautiful morning," Zurek smiles at everyone. "We just have some business to attend to. It won't take long." he waves towards the crowd dismissively. Facing the man on his knees,

Zurek lifts his chin. "Harrison Kreeft. We noticed that when you gave your tithe this month, you only gave seven percent, rather than the *preferred* fifteen. Why would that be?" he asks.

The man starts to shake. "Please, Mr. President. I have to feed my family. I didn't have enough this month," he trembles.

"Too many mouths to feed?" Zurek chuckles. "I can fix that," his expression changes in a second and he raises his hand. One of the men turns the safety off his gun.

"President Zurek please!" the man begs. "I need to care for my family! Please!"

"So, it should be one of your children then? Or maybe your wife?" he grins. The other Soldier turns his gun to the Kreeft family.

"No!" a cry rings out across the crowd. I look towards the voice and see Wren standing in front of the Kreeft kids. "We are at church! This is not the time or the place! Please!"

"Commander! Get control of your daughter!" Zurek shouts.

Commander Adler stomps over to Wren and grabs her by the arm, jerking her away from the kids. She tries to squirm away, tears filling her eyes. Before I can blink, the back of Adler's hand strikes Wren's cheek. She takes it like a champ. Her face goes blank and her hand slowly comes up to her cheek. Adler pulls her back to the family. Her oldest brother puts his arm around her and glares daggers at their father. Elissa doesn't look at her daughter.

"Which is it, Harry?" Zurek asks.

"Please ... don't hurt my children. Don't hurt my wife. I'll do anything. I pay anything. I'll pay double!" the man pleads.

"Don't make promises you can't keep," Zurek chuckles. "I think I have the perfect solution," he gasps. "Take the family. Gut their home," he commands the Soldier pointing the gun at the family. He turns his attention to the one with his gun on Kreeft. "Kill him," he growls.

"You're a monster!" his wife screams as her children are dragged away.

Another Soldier takes her. She kicks and screams the whole way. Wren watches after children sadly. I look back at Harrison Kreeft, on his knees, begging for his life. The crowd moves back and watches in horror as the Soldiers move away from him. The Soldier with the gun, who I know well, takes his aim and executes the man. Mother's hide their children, covering their eyes. I glance back at Wren again. A bruise is already forming, and more tears fill her eyes and spill down her cheeks.

"Everyone should return home." Zurek orders, leaving the man there, dead on the church lawn. I look down at Sonia. She looks disgusted but I feel nothing.

CHAPTER 3

"I really think we can trust him!" I whine.

"No! We know nothing about him! You barely know him!" Jamison shouts at me. I flinch. "He followed you. He's been watching you for weeks. Has he seen you come here?" he demands.

"No. I've made sure of that," I shake my head.

Jamison paces in front of me.

"I don't trust this, Wren. I have a very bad feeling in my gut. About all of it. He stood and did nothing at the church! He looked completely unbothered by what they did to that man and his family and what your father did to you! I do not think he is someone we can trust, especially not with you. The thought of anyone hurting you –"

"Mak won't hurt me. I can feel it. I know I can trust him. I would know if he wanted to hurt me," I insist. My instincts are never wrong. I wouldn't feel anything for him if he weren't one of us.

"Not yet. I can't risk exposing us yet. We aren't ready. We don't have the means necessary to protect ourselves if they attack," he sighs.

"Jamison! Why don't we just use what they have taught all of us and fight back if they attack?!" I demand and grab his jacket.

"That's not what we are about, Wren!" he snaps. "We are peace loving people. That's why we do what we do here. That's why we will wait." he tells me. "You cannot bring him here. That's the end of it," he adds and walks away from me.

I go home earlier that night. The only times I have been home before midnight is when I'm with Maksim, but I didn't want to be around Jamison anymore tonight. Jamison and Mary are an older couple that started the Reformation in this territory. They believe that peace will set us all free.

I believe in their reason for starting the resistance, but I wish they would get some damn guns and shoot the bastards. It would be a hell of a lot easier than linking arms and becoming martyrs when they do discover us. When I found them, they gave me hope. Everyone here did.

My father would have me hanged, publicly, if he knew. Jamison and Mary are like my parents away from real life. My brothers are all a part of this too. This is my family. It's something I want Maksim to be a part of. There is something about the way he focuses. His intensity is what we need.

The next day, I don't have the Academy, so I look up all the bakeries in town. I find the one that is owned by Sonia Ozera. It's in South Zone. Maksim said that she is like me, so maybe she wants something to do with the resistance? Maybe I can see if Maksim can be trusted.

"Hi, what can I get ya?" a girl with Mak's eyes and hair color asks me as I enter the small bakery.

I study her for a moment and then step closer to the counter.

"Are you Sonia Ozera?" I ask.

"Uhm ... yeah, who's asking?" she narrows her eyes at me. I don't know if I should just tell her my name. I doubt Maksim has actually talked about me.

"Uh … I'm Wren. Wren Adler," I tell her. Her eyes widen. "I know your brother. Is he here today?" I ask.

"Oh! No … he uh … he is off making deliveries … but uhm … he's talked about you." she rambles and smiles at me.

"Do you have a few minutes to talk?" I ask her.

She looks around her empty bakery.

"Yeah … one second," she goes to the door and puts up a "Be Right Back" sign and locks the door. "Come with me," she motions for me to follow her. We go back to an office and both sit down.

"This place is nice," I tell her, trying to make small talk.

"Thank you! What brings you here?" she asks.

"I am trusting my gut with this … I have some questions for you," I sigh. She nods. "How do you and Mak feel about the New World Order?" I ask.

She looks down.

"Our opinions differ. I'm no fan," she tells me.

"What about Mak? How does he feel? I mean … let's say there was a resistance. Would you guys support that?" I question.

Sonia closes her eyes tight and drops her head into her hands. Everything is quiet for a long time. Her knee shakes, and she shakes her head back and forth slowly. When she lifts her head, her eyes are watery, and she takes a deep breath.

"Wren … you need to listen closely. Please," she whispers. My heart is pounding in my chest. "I love my brother. He means well, he really does. He is obedient. He always has been. He doesn't want anyone to get hurt if they don't have to," her voice is thick with tears.

"Sonia, what's going on?"

"Maksim doesn't work for me. He's a N.W.O Central Soldier and he was assigned to follow you and get close to you, so you would lead him to the resistance. It's been his mission," she tells me. I feel like someone just hit me with a truck. "I don't know what he has told you. I don't know how he feels about doing this … but I know he intends to follow through with his orders. You have to get out of here, Wren. He's probably tracking your phone as we speak. Don't let him find you and the resistance," she warns me. We both stand. I am on the verge of tears and vomiting.

"Why … why are you helping me?" I stutter.

"I believe in what you are doing," she answers.

I pull my phone out of my pocket and slam it on the ground. With a cry, I stomp on it until it shatters and goes dead.

"What's going to happen to you for telling me?" I ask her. My heart is pounding in my chest.

"I'll be dying for a good reason," she smiles sadly and a tear falls. "I'm not going to run … but you are. Come on. You gotta go."

She pulls me out of the office and out to the bakery door. We both see Maksim walking across the street. Before Sonia can stop me, I burst out the door and meet Maksim in the street. He looks concerned and reaches for me. I back out of his reach and glare at him, unable to form words.

"Wren? What's wrong?" he asks. Sonia is behind me now. "What's going on? Why didn't you tell me you were coming here?" he questions.

I blink back tears and feel the ache in my throat.

"I trusted you," I whimper. His eyes shoot to Sonia, who puts her hand on my shoulder.

"I love you, Maksim … but I couldn't let you do this," she whispers.

His expression changes from concern, to anger.

"Sonia, what did you do?!" he yells.

"*Sonia*?" I spit. "Sonia told the truth!" I cry and suck in shallow breath. "She told me what's really been going on," I shake my head in disgust.

"Wren listen to me," he starts and grabs my shoulders. He pulls me closer to him and tries to rest his forehead on mine.

"No," I cut him off and shove him as hard as I can. "I'm done listening to your lies," I shake my head and start to back away from him more. "You made me believe that I meant something to you … but I'm really just a criminal. You're a lying *traitor*! I hope you're happy," I sob and turn on my heel, running away from town. I hear him shout my name, but I don't stop. I don't look back.

Guilt is like a brick in my chest. I wish Sonia would have come with me. Betrayal weighs me down completely. Sobs escape my throat as I run, but there is no time to stop and cry about it. I have to warn the Reformation. We have to get ready to stand our ground. Jamison isn't going to like this, but the time to act is now. If we aren't ready yet, we are about to be.

CHAPTER 4

Day after day, I go to Headquarters and follow through with each mission of the day, which are all centered around finding the resistance. After turning my own sister in for conspiring against the New World Order, I was promoted to a Commander and I have my own Soldiers to manage now. Jackson and I work closely together to find the rebels.

We believe they are amongst the commoners so together; we execute search warrants of every house, apartment and place of business. We confiscate electronic devices from every civilian, even fellow Soldiers. Anything that suggests disloyalty to the N.W.O results in the arrest and investigation of whoever the guilty party is. My bastard father has never been so proud of me, meanwhile, Sonia is being tortured in prison while she awaits her execution.

The days turn to weeks and slowly, the day comes. Mass execution of any and all proven of betrayal by way of hanging. The city is shut down for the entire day. No business is open. No one goes to work or the Academy. Everyone just waits until noon. Then, those who are still walking free make their way to center city where the platform and gallows are assembled. The crowd buzzes with a mix of energies. Many are just thankful it's not them or their family about to die. Other's supportive of the New World Order talk excitedly like it's some sort of sport. For a few, there is silence as they prepare to grieve the loss of loved ones.

While guilt rests in my chest like a sack of rocks, Commander Jackson's voice booms in the City Square. He stands on the stage with his fellow Commanders around him, except me. Because my sister is one of many that will be executed today, I have to watch from the crowd. I can't be there to say anything to her or give her any apologies. The prisoners are paraded onto the platform with bags over their heads and placed under every noose. As the bags are removed from their heads, I find Sonia in the middle of them all. My body is shaking with anger, fear, and grief. I didn't even have the chance to mess up this mission myself. She did it for me. Now, I have to watch her pay the price. I turned her in.

You turned in your own sister to be killed. If for nothing else, you will be going to hell for this.

Commander Jackson shouts to the growing crowd that these people are traitors. He describes each of their crimes. When he gets to Sonia, he says that she let a rebel get away which makes her one too. There's only one thing to do about rebels. They must be eliminated. My father stands at my side, face tense. I can't look directly at him. I can't look at anyone. I can only look at Wren's face on the white screens on stage. Under her face are those famous words. "Wanted! Dead or Alive". Behind the Commanders in Uniform sits the Executive Council. The President, Vice Presidents, and Secretaries sit in a row with their hands folded in their laps and their eyes on Commander Jackson. Wren's mother is easy to spot. Her hair is the same color, but she keeps it pinned back in a low twist. She has the same eyes, which are red and puffy. I can only assume from crying. Wren's father is among the Commanders on stage. His face is cold. I hate him. I hate him for reporting his own daughter. I hate him because he is the reason I was assigned this mission. I hate him for all of this.

This isn't his doing and you know it. This is all you.

"And now!" Jackson's voice brings me back to reality. "We will show those rebels who has the power!" he shouts. The crowd roars. My father claps stiffly. I want to shoot him for it.

I do nothing as I watch Commander Jackson backs away to the side of the platform and grasps the lever. The crowd is silent with anticipation. Hoods are removed and Sonia looks over at him, unafraid. Her eyes are focused on him. I see her lips move but can't hear what she says. Jackson's fist tightens around the lever and he spits at her feet, making some in the crowd cheer briefly. As he is about to pull the lever, a voice breaks through the city speakers.

"Stop!" a voice echoes. Jackson lowers his hand. The screens are no longer showing Wren's face. They are blank now. "Please!" the voice echoes again. Vice President Adler lets out a sob and sinks to her knees.

That's Wren's voice. "Think about what you are about to watch this man do! This is murder!" she says.

"They've tapped into the announcement system, sir," someone yells.

President Zurek stands calmly and walks to the middle of the stage.

"What do you criminals want?" he asks loudly.

"We are not the criminals! Look at what you're doing! The Reformation just wants peace," Wren's voice urges.

"The Reformation," he laughs. "Is that what you rebels are calling yourselves?"

"It's what we intend to be. If you murder these people … you'll give us no choice but to cut you off from every trading partner you have. Other cities have already started their Reformation process. Your people are not with you, President Zurek. This isn't the only New World Order Territory with a resistance on their hands," she tells him. We all watch him think for a long time.

"I assume I am speaking with Wren Adler," he sighs. There is no reply. "The Council will negotiate with your Reformation … but Wren Adler must come alone to the Council's Headquarters by 8 a.m. tomorrow." he says.

In the background, we hear a man begin to argue it, but is promptly shushed by Wren. There is another long silence.

"Let these people live," she pleads.

"They won't be harmed. For now."

"I'll be there, and I'll be alone. But when I get there, all of these prisoners must be released into the custody of The Reformation."

"You have yourself a deal," he agrees.

There is a screech and then the screens are projecting Wren's face again. I look at Sonia. She is looking at me from the stage, eyes cold and unfeeling. I shake my head as if to apologize for everything. She clenches her jaw and looks away from me.

My father grabs my shoulders and makes me face him. "Do not let yourself feel regret for being loyal to your people," he whispers firmly.

I nod and shrug him off. Sonia is personally taken away by Commander Jackson and the stage is cleared. Wren's face disappears from the screens and the crowd begins to filter out.

There is a melancholy feeling as the day passes on. I can't seem to shake the thought of Wren from my mind. My chest feels like it's being crushed by weights and my thoughts are scattered. There's something God awful about knowing I had the trust of someone so untrusting … and I broke it into pieces.

I find myself in the church, not long after leaving the square. I go to the pew where Wren and her family always sat. If I am doing the right thing, why do I feel so guilty? I look up at the cross behind the pulpit. Some part of me is hoping it will start projecting words of wisdom.

"Maksim Ozera," a voice echoes in the empty room. I turn and see Pastor Schulte walking towards me. "You are all the talk lately. I haven't seen you in Sunday services the past few weeks, but here you are, now," He smiles and sits beside me.

"I haven't felt right with God … and how can I sit in his house and listen to his word if I don't feel right with him?" I shake my head.

"Maksim … church and God's word is not for the saints. It's for the sinners. It's for those that don't feel right. His word gives guidance. It can bring peace if you allow it," he tells me.

I look down at the hymnal and feel a tug in my chest.

"I led someone to believe lies about me and those lies led them to trust me. I broke that trust and now my sister was going to be hanged for my lies."

"Have you asked for forgiveness?" He asks.

I open the hymnal and page through it.

"Who do I ask? Where do I even start?" I scoff.

"If you ask Him for forgiveness … it will come from your sister over time. But you have to ask. Our God is a merciful God. He will hear you," he pats my shoulder and stands.

"Thank you, Pastor," I mutter. "Can I ask you something?" I glance up at him. He nods. "Would you forgive me? If I lied to you … manipulated you and made you trust me, only for me to break that trust. Would you be able to forgive me?" I ask.

He looks down.

"Asking for forgiveness goes beyond just asking. There needs to be a change in action. Us humans … we don't care about what other's do and say. We care about how other's make us feel. If you want forgiveness, you have to be true and make other's feel your remorse. And then make a change," he answers.

I thank him again before he goes. I can't bring myself to leave right away. I stare down at the hymn that Wren knew by heart, even more than the others. I whisper the chorus to myself. "And he walks with me, and he talks with me, and he tells me I am his own."

I repeat those words to myself as I walk home, taking the long way. If I am ever lucky enough to see Sonia again, I will not miss the opportunity to tell her how sorry I am ... and I will make it up to her. If I ever see Wren again, I will be lucky if she doesn't try to kill me on the spot. If she doesn't... I have my work cut out for me.

The next morning, I get a call requesting my presence in the Council Headquarters. I know it can only mean one thing. It's after 8 a.m. When I get there, the place is surrounded by Central Soldiers. I walk past them and into the double doors. In the main room, the Council sits behind their half-oval desk. All are calm and collected. Even Wren's mother is composed, despite seeing her daughter with a gun in her hand, flailing it around as she makes demands, voice thick with hysteria.

She turns and when she sees me, she clicks the safety off the gun.

Just remember she was at the top of her class in firearms training.

I put my hands up and stop walking. She stares me down, eyes watery and shadowed by dark circles under them.

"Don't be an idiot," I hiss. "Turn the safety back on before you hurt someone."

"Stay back," she warns.

"Relax. I'm not here to try to stop you," I shrug.

"Then why are you here?" she demands. I look at the President.

"We called him here to stop you," Zurek shrugs. I let my hands drop and let out an irritated breath. "We let Sonia Ozera and the others go. What more do you want?" he asks Wren.

"I want your full attention," he growls.

"You have it, Wren. Put down the gun," her mom says shakily.

"The Reformation doesn't want to overthrow the New World Order. We want to make it better," Wren sighs and lowers the gun. "We want things to go back to the way they were ... before the War."

"Back to the way things were?" Zurek scoffs. "Child, you can't imagine the awful that was in this world before the War."

"I know there was art. There was music and literature. There was dance and theater. Those things gave people a will to live. The government wasn't killing people for having opposing beliefs!" she yells.

Zurek and some of the other's laugh.

"Not that you know of. Before the War, the government in this country was corrupt," he tells her.

"No … they weren't like this. They weren't forcing their ways onto others!" she shakes her head and grips the gun tighter.

"Just tell us what you and your little Reformation want from us. Do you all want to live? If you surrender, I will show mercy."

"No," she barks. "We will not back down. What you are doing … it's wrong. You're a murderer! All of you are! You need to back down! We will not," she insists.

Council members whisper and debate. Wren looks back at me, lowering her gun. Her eyes are cold, but I can see the hurt hiding behind the anger. I look away before I let my regret show. The doors behind me slam open. Wren raises her gun again. Commander Adler charges her.

Everything happens so fast. He tackles Wren and the gun goes off. The Council all ducks down. There is yelling. Everything gets loud, fast. The lights are shut off. At one point, I hear Wren scream. I am slammed to the ground and restrained before there is any time to react. The shouting continues, and more gunshots go off. Before I know it, I am unconscious.

I wake up in a damp, dingy room. I can hear water dripping slowly somewhere close by. As my eyes adjust, I see that I am in a cell. A prison cell. Not a N.W.O prison cell though. This is somewhere outside of the city.

The rebels …

"Mornin'," a voice murmurs from the dark corner of the cell.

"Where 'm I?" I groan.

"You, Solider are currently a prisoner in the Reformation bunker," the voice answers.

"What happened?" I sit up slowly.

He sighs. "It was a shit show. I sent backup with Wren. They were to hide unless she was in danger. When her dad charged in there like that … they acted. Soldiers and my men fought and … a lot of people died. Council members were caught in the crossfire. It wasn't pretty."

"Wren pulled the trigger," I mutter.

"I told her not to take that damn gun with her. I begged her. She wouldn't listen. When we saw that they called you in, we thought maybe everything would be okay. Maybe you would be able to talk sense into her. Clearly that didn't help the situation," he chuckles.

"Yeah, well … I'm the last person she wanted to see," I mumble, looking down.

"Alright, son, get off your pity horse. You're here, alive, for a reason," he stands up and comes into the light, smiling "I need your help."

"With?"

"You gon' get Wren back."

"We don't even know if she is alive," I shake my head.

"That's what you need to find out. If she is, you need to get her and bring her back here," he is an older man, like Commander Jackson. He has that same accent too.

"Why would you trust me to do that?" I ask.

He kneels down so we are eye level.

"Let me be clear. When I look at you, I see a lying traitor who hurt someone I care a great deal about. I don't trust you as far as I can throw you. But underneath all that, I know there has got to be some part of you that cares about that girl," his voice is low and threatening.

"What makes you think that?" I counter.

"Because no one is capable of walking into her life and walking out without loving her, at least a little," he whimpers. "Not even a cold-hearted bastard like yourself," he adds.

"What if she's dead?" I force myself to ask the question. As the words leave my tongue, a wave of nausea hits me like a truck.

"Then you get to live the rest of your miserable life knowing you are to blame," he answers.

"You can stop with the passive aggressive comments," I spit and stand up.

"Listen, boy," He grabs my throat and slams me against the stone wall. "You deserve everything that is coming your way. My comments should be the least of your concern," he snaps.

"I'll kill you, old man. Get your hands off me," I growl.

He doesn't even flinch. He's either not afraid of dying, or he is confident. Too confident.

"Find her," he orders and lets me go.

"She did this to herself! She was stupid enough to trust me," I choke out as I catch my breath. He grabs my shoulders, bending me down, and knees me in the stomach. I fall to the damp floor. "Just kill me," I spit at him. He grabs my hair and lifts my head to meet his eyes.

"That's too easy," he hisses and then connects his right fist with the left side of my face. "You're going to live with yourself," he adds and lets my head drop.

I lie there for a long time. I feel my body fill with anger and something else … I don't know. My skin begins to hurt. In a way, I am empty. It's like a big part of me is suddenly missing. I can't think about that feeling. *Focus on the anger.*

"Listen to me," I groan and push myself to my knees. "I know those people. I know those Soldiers. If they have her, they probably killed her already." I shake my head. His face falls. Instead of hitting me or snapping back with another insult, he starts to cry. Let me tell you, watching a grown man cry is just as pathetic as you might think.

He sinks to the floor and brings his knees up, rocking back and forth. The door opens, and an older woman comes in. She sinks beside him and puts her arms around him. I hear her whispering to him, calling him Jamison. He tells her that they might've lost Wren. She swipes the tears from her face. I sit there, unsure of what to do. Part of me wants to curl up in a dark corner and cry like I used to when mom died. I could never cry in front of Sonia or my father. I had to be strong for Sonia and my father would call me weak. I would go to my room and turn out all the lights, close the blinds and cry in the far corner of my room. That was different though. That was my mother. This … this is just a rebel.

Stop feeling. She's not worth it. You can't go soft. Not now.

"Please," The woman grabs my hand. I look at her. "I see it. I see what you feel. Please find her. Bring her back," She begs.

"Listen to me, woman," I sigh and look down. "She's most likely dead. You have to be prepared for that."

"Then bring us a body ... so we can bury her and grieve properly," she cries.

"I can't ... I can't do that," I shake my head. My voice is shaky.

"Why?" Jamison snaps.

"I can't carry that weight," I answer.

I don't have to explain to them what I really mean by that. Wren probably weighs next to nothing with her size. Anyone could carry her. A N.W.O Solider could carry three or four of her. It's a different kind of weight. It's the weight you feel in your soul. It's the kind that breaks your spirit more than your back. I almost let my own sister get executed. If Wren is dead ... I'll be forced to face what I am.

"Please," she sobs. I'm about to tell her I can't do that, but I stop myself. Instead, I hold her hands in both of mine and nod.

They take me out of the cell and up several flights of stairs. When we reach the top, Jamison opens a door which leads to a smaller room with a ladder going up. He tells me to go up the ladder and then I'll know where I am. I do as I am told. When I get to the top and open the door, I groan internally.

Beside me is the concrete slab tower. This bunker door was here the whole time. I close it softly. The sky is dark. I can't imagine it's earlier than midnight. The air is cold, and the wind is strong. It feels like a storm is blowing in. It'll probably be a blizzard. What a time for war.

The streets are empty. It's like ghost town at night. Usually bars are still open. Where is everyone? I make my way towards the Council Headquarters. In the basement, they have holding cells for those who will be executed. We don't have long term prisons.

I use my ID to get into the Headquarters. It's empty inside. Lights are off and every step echoes off the marble floors and walls. I go down the stairs to the basement and holding room. Every cell looks empty, but I hear shallow breathing. I pull out my phone for a flashlight. In the end cell, there is a small body curled up on the floor.

"Wren?" I whisper. The breathing continues, but the body doesn't move. "Wren is that you?" I press my face against the bars and shine the light on the body. Fawn colored hair covers their face, but I know that hair. It has to be her. "I'm getting you out of here," I mutter and search for something to pick the lock. "Wake up, Wren. You're okay." After multiple minutes of working on the lock, it pops open. I swing the door open and go to her, scooping her up in my arms. She's a little heavier than I would have imagined. I rush us up the stairs and into the main room. The moonlight gives me enough light to look at her closer. As her hair falls away from her face, I almost drop her. Instead I sink to my knees and lay who I thought was Wren down. She groans and looks up at me.

"Vice President Adler ... why were you down there?" I shake her.

She chokes and winces as she says, "I tried ... I tried to kill him." "Who?"

"Zurek," she lets her head fall to the side.

I shake her again.

"Where is Wren?" I demand.

She lets out a whimper and starts to cry weakly.

"They killed her. Shot ... she's gone," she cries. I feel my heart drop to my stomach. Without a second thought, I pick her up again and start running for the bunker.

It takes a lot longer to get back than it did to get to the Headquarters. Carrying Elissa Adler down the ladder and stairs became a significant struggle. My arms are burning and my legs ache. When I get back to the main floor of the bunker, Jamison and Mary run to me.

Let me be clear when I say bunker. This is an underground community. I imagine is was built before the New World Order gained power ... before the War even. It's huge and there are a lot of people here. People I labeled as criminals.

I tell them, "It's not her."

Jamison looks down at Elissa and frowns up at me.

"Is this ..."

"It's her mom. She tried to kill the President after ..." I trail off and look over at Mary. Her face falls. I swallow the lump in my throat and look back at Jamison. "I don't know this for sure ..." I start and take a deep breath. "We think they killed Wren. She says they shot her. I remember hearing lots of gunshots when everything went down."

Mary begins to sob and falls to her knees.

"But you said it yourself. We don't know for sure," Jamison says calmly.

"Where can I put her?" I glance down at Elissa, purposely ignoring what he said. I know those people ... she's probably dead. Jamison leads me to a room full of cots. He tells me that the doctors here will take care of her. When he and I are alone in a hallway, we stop walking.

"You can go back to your people now. We can do this without you," He crosses his arms.

I can't help but scoff at him.

"I'm not going back to them. I can't," I shake my head. He looks surprised. "I've been missing and now one of their prisoners is gone. They'll torture me until I provide a valid alibi for my disappearance. And besides ... you were right," I shrug and bite the inside of my cheek to keep from frowning too noticeably. "About feeling something," I add.

"I don't think she's dead, Soldier. I would feel it," he tells me and pats his chest lightly.

I look down and nod.

"Then where is she?" I ask.

He puts his hand on my shoulder and says, "That's what we are going to find out." I nod again. "Get some rest, Solider," he sighs and starts to walk away from me.

"It's Maksim," I call after him. "I don't think I'll ever be a soldier again. If I go back now ... I'll always be a traitor, even if they don't know it ... which they will. They always find out exactly what you don't want them to," I tell him.

He smiles back at me, almost knowingly.

"Still ... once a soldier, always a soldier," He winks and continues to leave me.

The following weeks are like Hell on Earth. The Reformation's technology is incredible, but when I learned that they don't intend on using weapons, I lost a lot of faith. On the bright side, with the technology available, we were able to hack into the city's cameras. The city is on curfew. It's Hell for them too. A lot of people have left to come to the resistance. A lot of people have died for rising up. Another bright side is Sonia is alive and well here. She isn't talking to me though. I wouldn't either. I asked for her forgiveness. She says I have it, but she hasn't seen a change in me yet. Schulte said there needs to be a change. I'm fighting for that change. I'm going against everything I ever believed in.

A lot of people here don't trust me. They have no reason to. Not yet. My own mind has been the worst part. Jamison still believes Wren is alive, but I am losing hope. There is no sign of her. Nothing. It's like she never existed. They have "Wanted" poster with Elissa's face on them now. She's been well. They did some damage on her. She said she was publicly beaten after trying to kill the President. She was going to be executed the morning after I found her. As every day passes, I find it harder to get out of my new bed. I blame myself for everything. I don't even need to pay attention to those who call me a murderer and the Devil himself. I hear it all from myself. Being around these people … their hearts are rubbing off on me. Now is not the time to be weak.

Wren was a big deal around here. I mean, I'm not exactly surprised. Jamison tells me that she was going to be the face of the Reformation. He said that she had a presence in every room she entered. Somehow, everyone was always smaller than her. She commanded the attention of everyone she addressed. She didn't bully people into listening. She just … spoke and she had everyone on a hook. Looking back at our too brief time together … I believe it. She always had a hook in me. I probably didn't even know it most the time.

At night, I lie awake feeling empty while at the same time, being filled with guilt. I'm not used to guilt. I've never let myself feel this way. I feel so ridiculous. I barely knew her … but also knew so much. She was complicated but also so easy to see through. I can't explain what she was. She was beautiful … I know that much. Not just on the outside. Her soul was beautiful too. She saw the good in me. It takes someone special to see past what I am.

You weren't really you with her. You lied to her. You were fake.

CHAPTER 5

"Maksim!" Sonia yells and shakes me awake. I don't know if she's about to punch me or what. She stands beside my cot, waiting for me to fully wake up.

"What's wrong with you?" I growl.

"You have to see this," she tells me. Her eyes are wide with hope and horror. Worst combo ever.

I jolt out of bed and follow her to the TV room. On the center TV, City Square is focused in. The stage is up again. There is no Council. Only President Zurek and Soldiers stand on the stage. In front of them, Wren sits on her knees. Her skin is bruised, and her cheeks are sunken in. Her head sags and there is no fight left in her eyes."She's alive," I mutter.

She snaps at me. "They are going to execute her, Maksim."

"Not if our guys get there in time," Jamison says from the doorway. We both look back at him. "I sent a team. They are going to get her. We ain't losing this battle. Not with her," He shakes his head.

"What if they don't make it?" I ask.

"They'll make it. Zurek is going to make a big speech," he says confidently.

Surely enough, Zurek is babbling away about order and the good that the N.W.O does. Occasionally, one of the Soldiers will hit Wren, making the crowd cheer. Zurek doesn't stop once. His beady eyes make my skin crawl. Seeing what they have done to her makes me sick. I hate myself for ever being a part of them.

"Look at her," Sonia whispers.

"They've been torturing her." I tell her.

She looks at me, disgusted.

"I'm sure you would know," she spits. She isn't wrong. I've tortured people before.

"The bruises … they're everywhere. She's been beaten. Starved. I doubt she has her nails. They usually rip them off, one by one," I tell her.

"Why are you saying all of this?!" she demands.

I look down at her and force my jaw to unclench before replying.

"Saying it out loud makes it impossible to ignore that this is my fault. What they did to her … is my fault." "Why are you pretending to care about someone all of the sudden?" she asks.

"I wish I was pretending," I grumble and look back at the screen.

Sonia prays quietly beside me. She prays for strength and protection for Wren. She prays for the people there to rescue her. Sonia has always been better than me at having unfailing faith. I could use that right now.

Zurek almost done with his little speech. "This is a symbol of new beginnings for us," he bellows, standing with his fancy suit and perfect, holier-than-thou posture.

On other cameras, we see the team start to move into place. Elissa comes in and watches with us. I fear that she will have to watch her daughter get executed. Zurek calls Commander Adler to the stage.

"No …" Elissa cries. She grabs my arm with one hand and covers her gaping mouth with the other. Sonia puts her arm around Elissa. I hold her hand and we stare at the screen in horror.

"And now!" Zurek beams. "A message to those who wish to stand against the New World Order," he motions to Commander Adler. *Don't tell me he is about to shoot his own daughter.*

He raises his gun to Wren's head. Elissa begins to sob. Sonia holds her up and hugs her for support. I let go of her hand and get closer to the screens. On the rooftop across from the stage is a sniper. One of our guys. I look over at Jamison.

"I thought you didn't believe in violence," I mumble.

"I won't regret this. Not for her," he answers.

Commander Adler is about to pull his trigger, when our sniper fires. As soon as the snipers bullet meets Adler's head, Adler pulls his trigger. Elissa lets out a scream as Wren falls. His bullet hit her awfully close to the heart. It's hard to tell. The sniper continues to fire as other resistance members charge the stage, creating distractions. One grabs Wren and makes their way out of the square with her. Everyone else follows suit. The waiting is the worst part. After the team got back with Wren, they immediately took her into surgery. The doctors knew that her life was hanging by a thread. She was already weak. They have valuable resources here, but it's no hospital.

After almost two hours, the main surgeon comes out of the medical room. Elissa, Jamison and Mary all stand immediately. I sit with my fists clenched in my lap. The doctor looks down and sighs. Sonia reaches over and covers my fists with her hand.

"It's not looking good. We have her on oxygen and an IV … but we couldn't get the bullet. It's too close to her heart to risk. We don't have the skills or supplies we need to get it out. It's going to take some time to heal, but she needs to gain strength. Strength that she doesn't have right now," he explains.

"Is she awake? Is she okay?" Elissa asks.

He shakes his head. "She's not awake. She's barely hanging on. This can go one of two ways."

"But as of right now … she's alive," Jamison says.

"At this point in time, yes, but she is on supplies that we don't have much of. Oxygen and fluid. We need more of a lot of things if she is going to pull through," the doctor tells him.

"Make me a list and I'll make it happen," Jamison replies.

"Can we see her?" I blurt out. Everyone looks at me.

"I don't see why not," he shrugs and leaves.

After everyone else is done visiting her, I go in. I wear a mask and gloves and keep my distance for a while. I just look at her. She looks so different. Her pale skin is greyer now. She is covered in bruises and scars. Her eyes have the darkest circles under them. She looks like a ghost. I force my feet to move closer. A single tear escapes my eye. I lean closer and pull down the mask just long enough to tell her how sorry I am. God, I want nothing more than for her to hear me.

Life in the bunker is mind numbing. We sit behind the screens and watch the city live. The only thing that Jamison is having anyone do it look for oxygen tanks and water. He hardly leaves Wren's side. Her waiter friend is a part of the Reformation. He won't look at me. No one will. Not directly. Sonia is starting to talk to me now. Not without bitterness, but she does talk. Sometimes we sit on the concrete tower at sunset and watch the world go dark. It's the closest we get to the old days. Back before mom died ... before I joined the N.W.O. Back when we were best friends.

"Do you think Wren will pull through?" I ask Sonia while we are on watch on the concrete tower. No one comes out here much, but the rebels like to be prepared if any N.W.O soldier comes snooping around.

"Is that why you've been pouting?" she counters.

"I'm going nuts. Thinking about anything happening to her ..." I shake my head and look down. "It's my fault," I force myself to say it. "And knowing that actually hurts which is... new."

"I never thought you would be the type to lose your mind over a girl."

"Neither did I," I chuckle. "I guess that's why it sucks so much, ya know? I can't get her out of my head. It's ridiculous. We barely know each other."

"I think you two figured each other out pretty fast," she shrugs. I look over at her. "She's smart ... and you have access to very confidential information about people. I don't think it's too outrageous to assume that maybe not all of the emotions were fake. There's no controlling that."

"So, I'm not crazy?"

"Well, I wouldn't say that," she grins before pausing for a long time. "I don't know what to tell you, Maksim. The only time I saw you two together, she was crying and running away." she chuckles as she looks out at the sunset. It's just like when I met Wren. It feels like yesterday, but it was almost three months ago now.

I don't have time to fire back at Sonia. The bunker door opens, and Peter looks up at us. He looks out of breath.

"What's your problem?" I snap.

He glares at me. "Wren is awake," he tells us.

I am off that tower and in that bunker faster than the bullet that hit her. Sonia is right behind me. Peter leads us into the medical room. Wren is sitting up with her back to us. She looks like a skeleton. I stop in my tracks, not sure if I can face her right now. Peter goes in ahead of me. I wish he wouldn't, but I force myself to follow. When her eyes fall on me, they turn icy. Sonia hugs her lightly and then Peter steps forward. Wren smiles at him weakly and hugs him too.

"How do you feel?" Peter asks her.

"Like I've been tortured, shot, and in a coma for two weeks," she answers and glares at me.

"Wren …" I step forward. Before I can blink, her fist connects with my jaw. Everyone gasps. I look down and nod, knowing I deserved that. "Feel better?" I glare back at her.

"Don't you *dare* look at me like that," she snaps. "Everything that has happened is because of you. You have put so many people in danger. You caused so much pain!"

I reach for her. She backs away. "Wren, we need to talk. I'm so sorry for all of this, but you need to hear me out," I run my hands through my hair in frustration and try another step closer.

Sonia steps between us. "Maksim," she hisses, but Wren is already trying to lung. Peter tries to hold her back.

"I don't need to do anything!" she screams. Her voice is raspy and raw. Tears stream down her face. She's hurt.

"I think you need to leave," Peter says.

"Let me go," she shoves him away. "Get out. All of you," she sits down on the bed and takes slow deep breaths.

"She needs to rest," he starts to usher us out.

"She means you too," I growl at him. As we are leaving, Elissa runs past us and embraces Wren. I force myself to walk away from that room.

Why do I even care? Just let her pout. When I am finally alone in a hall, I slam my fist into the wall and stifle a scream. I sink to the concrete floor and bite my sleeve. She makes me feel. She makes me feel everything and I don't like it. I just want her forgiveness, if nothing else. I can't focus knowing I've hurt her like this.

Stop. Let it go.

Tears spill onto my cheeks. My hand begins to swell and throb. Sonia comes around the corner and I swear under my breath as her expression turns to concern.

"Maksim …"

"Get away from me," I swipe the tears away from my eyes.

"Are you crying right now? Listen, she just needs time," she sits in front of me.

"It's not that," I laugh and shake my head. She looks at my hand and sighs.

"You're an idiot," she growls and makes me stand up. We go to her room and she cleans my hand, then wraps it. "She'll forgive you with time," she whispers.

"It doesn't matter," I mutter.

"You have to let her heal. Physically and emotionally," she tells me.

"I know, Sonia. Listen we have other things to worry about now. Bigger things," I stand up and move towards the door.

"Right," she sighs. "But Mak … it's okay to feel this way," she adds. I turn and leave.

Days pass. I force myself to focus on what mission lies ahead. Jamison no longer cares about peace or negotiation. He wants to take The New World Order down for what they have done. I like it better this way. He's speaking my language. Step one is building our weapon supply.

It has been easier to ignore the pain in my chest with everything else that is going on. Wren isn't involved in anything yet. She has been on bed rest mostly. I've only tried to talk to her twice. The first time was a crash and burn. The second time was tense, but she didn't tell me to screw off again. I've gained Jamison's trust. He has sent me on missions with the other teams and I am grateful for something to do other than sit around and soak in my own self-pity. Sonia is better with me. A lot of people are since Wren has been awake. She's become best friends with Sonia. Makes me wonder if I stand a chance.

I get back from a weapon gathering mission late one night and pass the medical room. I notice someone sitting on the edge of Wren's bed with her. I stop and watch from the shadows. I assume it's Peter. He's been attached to her let a shadow. I watch from the hall.

"Listen … I've messed up. I should have never put my hands on you. I can't apologize enough. You deserve better than what I gave you," he says.

"I know, Jeremy. You don't need to tell me that," Wren responds coldly.

Jeremy? Are you kidding me? You have got to be kidding me.

"The Academy was tearing everyone apart in the final year. It took everything I was ... and it tore us apart. Wren, I will never do that to you again. We are both away from that now."

"You could have killed me," she shakes her head.

"What about the two years before that? Two years, Wren," he reaches for her hand. She lets him hold her hand in his.

How is she letting him touch her?

"Wren, I came here for you. I deserved everything you did to me. You should have killed me," he chuckles.

Damn right.

"I wanted to," she mutters, looking down.

"But you didn't. You're better than that. Look at what you've done here. You've built a following greater than the New World Order Army," he smiles. He's got one of those smiles that radiates confidence. He thinks he's the best thing.

"I know what I've done, Jeremy. What I've done is everything you told me I would never be able to do," she snaps.

He sighs.

"I was wrong. I see that now. I'm asking for your forgiveness. Nothing more. Just ... your blessing to be here and be a part of this," he says hopefully.

Please say no. I can't keep up my good behavior if this guy is around.

"You're forgiven. But you're on thin ice, Jeremy, I swear to all that is Holy if you take one misstep ... I *will* kill you," she threatens, but he doesn't seem phased. He stands up and kisses the top of her head, making my stomach turn and my throat close.

"You won't regret this."

Lord, give me strength.

CHAPTER 6

"Get up! We gotta go!" Sonia shakes me awake. I am very quickly on my feet and searching for my boots in the dark.

"What happened?" I demand as I shove my feet into the boots and tie the laces tight. My fingers stumble with the laces and my eyes feel heavy still.

"They know where we are. They are on the move. We have to evacuate. Pack your things," she tells me and leaves my small room.

I shove my few clothing items and even fewer possessions into a backpack and pull it onto my back. I go out to the hallway where others are doing the same. People are panicking. Everyone is rushing around. It seems like we are to meet in the common room and all leave together. I get there and find Jamison. He is flustered and angry. He tells a bunch of us to get the weapons we have collected.

Jeremy is one of the ones to come with us to the storage room. I'm sure he knows who I am at this point. I doubt Wren kept whatever we were a secret. He gives me side glances and when I look back at him, he'll smile slightly and look away.

Don't bust his teeth out. Don't bust his teeth out.

She's made her choice. If she wants to be an idiot, let her be an idiot.

You shouldn't care anyway. It's over. There is no hope of getting back in her good grace's. Just let it go. You are being weak.

This is war. Jeremy and I are on the same side. I can't let it be personal. I can't let any of this be personal anymore. I'm going to have to kill my former friends. Who knows what they think. They might know I am a traitor. They might think I am dead. No matter what they think or know ... I am the enemy now and they are all going to know that very soon. At this point, no side would be better than this. "Maksim!" Sonia yells for me as I shove another gun in a duffle bag. I look back at her. "Come on! Leave the rest!" she pleads. People are starting to evacuate.

I look over at Jeremy. He's already looking at me. There is still a lot of ammunition and guns here. Leaving them would be a huge waste. He practically reads my thoughts and keeps shoving guns and ammo into bags.

I look back at Sonia.

"Go. We will catch up," I tell her. She glares and shakes her head at me, but heads for the stairs.

"We'll make it," Jeremy yells to me over the chaos. I glance at him. "You were a Solider right?" he asks.

I zip up one bag and start packing another.

"Yeah," I reply shortly.

"Wren says you were probably one of the best," he says as he looks away from me. I stop and look straight ahead at the wall.

"Why would she say that?" I growl.

"Probably because they assigned you to her. And the mission you had. They wouldn't give that to just anybody," he chuckles.

I look back down.

"It's only because I was young and could get close to her," I grumble.

"Well it worked," he scoffs. My eyes shoot over at him. He stops packing and looks at me. "I just mean you did get close. She let you in. She probably would be with you right now … if you didn't royally mess things up," he smiles and shakes his head.

I grab the last bit of ammo and close that bag too, then look at him. I can feel my body burning with rage and the overwhelming urge to shoot him.

"Just remember you messed up too, Jeremy. I *never* put my hands on her," I snap.

"So, you've done your research," he snorts as we begin to leave. "You're right. I messed up too. But I didn't get her captured and tortured. I didn't almost get her killed."

"You really don't know when to shut up," I hiss.

"She talks in her sleep. Did you know that?" he asks as we reach the top of the stairs.

I stop at the ladder and look back at him.

Why is he there when she's asleep?

"So?" I shrug.

"At first it bothered me when I would hear her saying your name. Calling for you. It really bothered me. Then I remembered that I was the one she didn't mind being around anymore. I was there, at her bedside … not you. And if she *really* wanted you there, she would ask," he smirks.

It takes everything within me to not break his jaw. I grip the ladder bars and start to climb.

Lie. Don't let him see it tears you a part.

"Good for you. Forgiven after what you did. That's huge. I mean you guys were together a while. Two years is a long time," I reply tightly. We reach the top and start following after the others. "It's a lot of time for someone to grow up too," I mutter and start running for the group.

I look back and see Mak and Jeremy running after us. They are carrying the ammo. My stomach twists seeing them together. Running is exhausting as it is. When there is a bullet inside you, right against your heart, it sucks a little more. All that and then seeing two of the people that once meant so much to you before hurting you, running side by side.

"Where are we going?" I yell up to Jamison.

He yells back, "South. One of the territories has already been overthrown by our people. It should be safer there."

"Should be?" Sonia breathes heavily beside me. Her and my mom and holding my arms to keep me going.

Most people are in front of us. Jamison has Peter and some other young members leading the way. The old and weak are in the back like me. Minus Sonia and my mother. Jeremy and Maksim catch up with us and slow their pace to match ours. Maksim doesn't look at me. Jeremy takes Sonia's place, allowing her to join Maksim. She grabs his arm and pulls him in front of us. My mom gives Jeremy a glare before pushing forward to keep up with the group. My legs ache and my chest burns, but I keep pushing myself forward. We have to get as far away from here as possible. I won't be the reason we have to stop. I will not be the reason we get caught.

We travel for an entire day. By late the following night, we make it to the Territory south of us. Jamison was right. It was overthrown. It's practically a ghost town. A few men greet us at the center of the city. They talk with Jamison and Mary while the rest of us wait is a cluster. I legs are shaky. My heart is pounding in my chest and everything hurts. Maksim is watching me from a distance. Jeremy and my mom keep me standing. I see Jamison look back at us occasionally and motion to me. He's probably explaining what happened. I feel myself start to sink. My mother and Jeremy's voices are distance.

The las thing I see is Maksim rushing over to us and then everything is black.

CHAPTER 7

"Get your hands off of me!" I shove him away from me and try to go into the hospital room where Wren lies, half awake. Her mother is with her right now.

"She doesn't want to see you! You're nothing more than a traitor!" Jeremy shoves back.

"You wound me," I hiss sarcastically.

"You know I'm right," he counters. I push past him and walk in the room.

Elissa and Wren look at me. Wren's face is ashy again, but her cheeks still flush up. Elissa looks down at her and squeezes her hand.

"It's okay, mom. Give us a few minutes," she says. Her voice is shallow and weak. My chest clenches at the sound of it. Elissa walks past me, smiling softly as she leaves the room and closes the door. I stand there for a moment, just looking at her. "Are you going to talk or what?" she snaps.

I force my feet to push me closer to her. I sit down in the chair where her mother was sitting.

"*We* need to talk. Not just me," I sigh. She glares at me. "I'll start by apologizing. Again. No number of times will ever be enough. But I can't do my job here effectively until I know that you forgive me. We can at least be civil with each other."

"You hurt me," she whimpers. Tears glisten in her eyes.

I swallow the lump in my throat.

"I know. But I'm not willing to say that I regret taking on the mission," I shake my head.

"Why?" she demands.

"I would have never met you if it weren't for the mission. And I never would have found a way out of the N.W.O. If I were smart... I would have done things the right way."

"I trusted you. And you broke that trust, big time."

"I know."

"How am I supposed to just trust you again?" she begins to cry.

"I would never ask you to," I whisper. There is silence for a long time. I can't bring myself to look at her. The disappointment on her face ... it's painful.

"I can forgive you," she wipes her tears away.

"Thank you, Wren," I let out a breath of relief.

"But if you ever lie to me again ... about anything. You're done," she adds. I lean forward and nod. She swallows and looks down at her hands. "You made me feel like I was worth something. Like what I had to say was worth listening to," she looks at me again.

"That wasn't a lie," I tell her and stand up. I start towards the door and then stop. I look back at her. "Don't let yourself take steps backwards. Keep looking forward. There is a lot to look forward to," I smile slightly and walk out. Jeremy glares at me as I walk down the hallway and out the double doors.

I go out to the empty street. Loose papers blow with the winter breeze. The new year has come around. There was probably a celebration back where we are from. As much of a celebration as the N.W.O is capable of. There was nothing here. Wren is in the hospital and the others are preparing to fight. This Reformation group has a lot more supplies than we did. We might actually stand a chance now.

Today is especially stressful for everyone. Wren is going into surgery soon. They think they have the tools they need to get the bullet out of her. It's going to be a long, hard surgery for all the doctors involved. I am going to stay far away from the hospital.

I go to my assigned apartment. I live with Sonia here now. When I get inside, she is making lunch. She smiles at me and then sits a plate in front of me on the counter. I'm not really sure what I am looking at.

"What is this?" I ask and sit on the stool.

"I'm not really sure. I just threw what we had together," she grins

I start eating the mess on the plate. I wouldn't say I like it, but I eat it because one, it's food and two, it makes Sonia happy. I owe her for a lot of years of misery. I should have stood up to our father when he would talk to her the way he did. I should have stood with her, rather than against her. I should have never let them take her and try to kill her. Wait …

What is that sound? You know that sound. Get out. Get out.

"Sonia …" I gasp. She looks over at me, mouth full. "We have to go. Get out," I grab her hand. She coughs and jerks away from me.

"What is your problem?" she chokes at me.

"Planes. Planes are coming. They are flying low. It's an attack," I tell her. As the sound comes closer, her eyes get wide.

We run out our door and down the three flights of stairs to the ground floor, yelling to get people out. We run outside and look up. Three planes with "N.W.O" painted in bold on them are flying this way. I was right. They are low, and they are bomber planes. One is headed directly for the hospital.

Wren. Get to her. Get her out of there.

The city alarm starts going off. People run outside from every shop, apartment and business building. They look up and scream. Sonia and I are running for the hospital. The leader here comes on the loud speaker. He is telling people to get to the bunkers.

"Maksim! We won't make it in time!" Sonia yells and slows to a jog.

I look back at her.

"Get to a bunker. I will find you. I have to make sure she gets out okay," I shake my head. She nods and pulls me into a hug. I haven't had a hug in years. I think the last hug I ever got … was from mom. Sonia never hugged me after that because we spent most of our time arguing.

"Don't die," she whispers before running towards one of the bunkers.

Bombs begin to drop around us. They shake everything. I stumble into the doors. People are running out. I hope they didn't start her surgery yet. We are so screwed if they did. I see Elissa trying to carry Wren all by herself. I push through other people to get to them. I don't see Jeremy anywhere. If he left them … Wren has to see who he really is. I'm still here. Like Pastor Schulte said … make a change.

"Elissa!" I yell as I reach them. "Did they start the surgery?" I ask and take Wren from her arms. She's boney and frail. She couldn't have been like this before being tortured. I look down at her and pray that they didn't start the surgery.

"No. They just put her under and then the planes came. She's knocked out," Elissa tells me as we start to run from the building.

"Where's Jeremy?" I ask as we get outside.

"He left. He said he needed to do something, right before the planes came," she growls. I stop walking and look down at Wren. He left them before the planes came and didn't come back for them. "Come on," she tugs my arm toward the nearest bunker entrance.

A bomb drops and sends us flying back. I cling to Wren. She moans and starts to wake up. I scoop her up again and go towards Elissa. She gets to her feet and we go around the fire to the bunker entrance. We make it in and the door closes behind us. We go through the second door and down steep stairs. When we get into the bunker, everyone else there looks at us. People are huddled together as bombs drop, shaking the dim lights. There are cots that people are sitting on. Three guys stand up from theirs and motion me over with Wren.

She's a big face around the Reformation here. I lay her down and cover her with the thin sheet. We all sit around, waiting. It's like the bombs never stop. Wren comes to a few times, but each time sinks back into sleep. Her mother strokes her hand and puts her arm around her every time a bomb hits. I keep my head down and wait to hear the planes flying away.

After what feels like ages, the bombs stop falling and the plane's engines start to fade away. We here the "all clear" siren sound twice. Everyone else emerges from the bunker. Elissa and I take up the back with Wren in my arms. When we get to the surface, we gasp and look around in awe. Fires are everywhere. A bunch of people are already working on putting them out. There are bodies scattered around. I feel sick to my stomach. Something doesn't feel right.

"Elissa ... can you take her back to the hospital –" I stop when I see that the hospital is crumbling. I look towards my apartment. It's not even touched. "Go to my apartment. Third floor, last door on the left," I hand her my keys and Wren.

Once she's gone, I start searching for Sonia. She would have found me by now. I am asking people and looking frantically. I find Jamison on his knees over a body.

"Jamison?" I mutter and go around. He's holding Mary's lifeless body, sobbing. I sink beside him. "I'm so sorry," I breathe.

"Maksim …" he croaks and looks at me, eyes empty. I search his face for something. Anything. He points, and I follow his finger. I see a body laying … in the same clothes as Sonia was earlier. I stumble over and fall to my knees.

Sonia lies with blood covering her face and arms. Blood seeps through her shirt from her stomach. I pull her head onto my lap.

"So-Sonia?" I whimper. My voice catches in my throat. She looks at me, but she isn't seeing me. Her eyes are blank.

The corner of her mouth turns up slightly and blood gurgles in her throat as she says, "Hey little brother."

"You're going to be okay. I'm going to get you to a doctor," I start rambling. Tears are dripping down my cheeks and onto her face and shirt. I wipe them off of her. Her blood covers my hands.

"Mak …" she whispers. "It's over," She shakes her head.

I cringe.

"Sonia, shut up. Don't say that," I snap. I put pressure on her stomach where the blood is coming from. "I've got you. I've got you," I mumble. She grips my hand. I look around for a doctor. "Help!" I shout.

"I always … always knew you-you would be an amazing man. You're so great," she cries. I shake my head to keep her words away. "I'm so proud of you."

"Sonia? Please don't go. I need you. I need you to kick my ass when I am being an idiot," I cry.

"I love you, Maksim," she coughs. Blood spots her lips. "I want to see mom," She smiles at the sky. I feel like my insides are being ripped out as I resist the urge to vomit. My stomach is twisting and turning. My throat is tight. It hurts. My head and heart are pounding faster than ever before.

"Yeah?" I sniffle and look away from her dying eyes. "I do too … but you can't yet. You're not dead, Sonia," I whisper.

"I can't wait to hug her again," she smiles more. I have nothing to say. After a long silence, her smile fades and she looks at me deep in the eye. "Do right by the rebellion. For me … please," she croaks before her head falls to the side.

"Sonia?" I shake her. "Sonia, come on," I beg. "No … come on. Come on," I start doing chest compressions, knowing it won't make a difference. I can't help but let out an agonizing scream. I swear at the sky. I swear at the New World Order. I swear at myself for ever being a part of them.

I rock back and forth holding her body in my arms. I can feel it getting cold. I can't stop the sobs from escaping from my throat. A few people put their hands on my back and shoulders as they pass by. Every touch feels like an iron rod just pulled from a fire. I beg her to come back. Around me, people identify the other bodies that lay dead. Sonia's blood soaks through my clothes. It's on my face, hands and shirt. I hold her closer. As far as family goes, she was all I had left. My father knew that we were here. He knew that our lives were at risk and he did it anyway. But … how did he know we were here? How did they find us? We left by foot … someone must've told them.

They killed her. Those bastards killed her.

That night, I didn't go back to my apartment. I slept in the street outside the crappiest bar I've ever seen. I wasn't the only one. A lot of us were grieving. I'm not proud. Those who say they drink to forget … well I don't blame them. The stuff works. All of us who were in the bar were telling our "war stories" one minute and the next, we were laughing about anything and everything.

The next morning, I stumble to my apartment and into the living room. I flop back on the couch and look down at Sonia's blood staining my skin. Elissa comes out of my bedroom. She sits beside me and holds my blood covered hand.

"I heard about Sonia," she says softly. Hearing her name is like a gunshot going off right beside my head. "You should get cleaned up," she sighs. I nod numbly and go to my room to get clean clothes. Wren is asleep in my bed, still in the hospital gown.

"Here," I mutter and toss a pair sweatpants and a long sleeve on the bed. "She might want something warmer when she wakes up. I won't be long," I tell her. My voice is hoarse. My mouth tastes like blood and bad decisions.

I stand in the shower and let the hot water wash away Sonia's blood, but it won't wash away my regret and anger and … complete sorrow.

After a really long time of silently sobbing in the shower, I get out and dressed in clothes that aren't covered in blood.

Wren is just waking up when I come out of the bathroom. Elissa is telling Wren what happened. I keep my eyes down as I throw my old clothes in the trash. I'm not even going to bother with them. Wren looks over at me, tears spilling onto her cheeks. I can't look her in the eye. Her lips are parted in shock.

"Mak ..." she whimpers. I hold my hand up and turn my head away from her.

"You can go get cleaned up if you would like. You two are welcome to stay as long as you need," I mumble and leave the bedroom. I go over to Sonia's room and slam the door closed.

I hear the shower turn on and I hear Elissa in the kitchen. I sit on Sonia's unmade bed and bite my sleeve to stifle a sob. I hate this. I hate everything. I hate that I was ever a part of the New World Order. I hate that I went on that mission. I hate that I let Sonia get mixed up in all of this. I wish I could take everything back. Just become a commoner. She begged me to be a commoner like her. I could have prevented all of this.

I spend hours in that room, curled up on her bed, crying like a baby as quietly as I can. I hate myself for that. Last time I did this was when mom died. I was younger then. This Reformation is making me soft. Jamison would say it's better to feel pain rather than feel nothing at all. I disagree. I rather go back to feeling nothing.

There is a light tap on the door, pulling me out of my own head.

"Maksim?" Wren calls softly. I'm sitting up now, all cried out. I've just been staring out the window at the fallen city. "Mak, I'm coming in," she sighs and opens the door.

"Get out," I grumble, barely glancing at her. My sweatpants and long sleeve hang on her.

"No," she crosses her arms and plants her feet. She's stubborn. She doesn't like to be controlled. I know this, so why do I bother?

"I don't want you here, right now, Wren," I snap and look over at her. Her eyes are red and puffy from crying. Her nose is red, and her face is splotchy.

"You aren't the only person who lost someone today," her voice shakes.

"I'm not saying I did," I lay back and stare at the ceiling, prepared to get a lecture about how Jeremy is missing right now. I don't want to sound like an insensitive ass, but that jerk is nothing like my Sonia. Losing him isn't a big loss to Wren, if he's even dead. She's probably better off.

"My brothers were on their way here," she blurts out. I sit up and look at her again. I see her body begin to shake slightly and fresh tears make their way to the surface of her eyes. "The second oldest ... Mason ... he was shot, and my other two brothers had to leave him there. They didn't even get to bury him," she whispers and wipes her face with my sleeve. "And now they are on their way ... just two of them ... to find out that Mary is dead. Jeremy is gone, I don't even know where. Their friends are dead, and our brother is dead," she cries. "I know you're in pain, but don't act like you're the only one," her voice catches in her throat and the tears really start to spill. She doesn't even bother trying to stop them.

I say nothing. I can't form words for so many reasons, it's driving me insane. She looks down and leaves, slamming the door behind her. I force myself to stand up and go after her. When I open the door, she is already leaving the apartment. Her mom looks at me from the kitchen counter and smiles sadly. Her eyes are bloodshot too.

"I'll go get her," I tell her and go after Wren.

I catch up with her out in the street. She's barefoot. There's broken glass and gravel everywhere.

"Wren," I hiss and grab her arm.

She turns and swings at me.

"Get off of me!" she sobs. I catch her swinging arm by the wrist and pull her closer. She squirms and tries to pull away. I let her go, holding my hands up.

"You're acting like a child," I growl.

"I need some air and space! Please, just leave me alone," she runs her hands through her hair.

"You're barefoot. There's broken glass everywhere. You stormed out like a toddler throwing a tantrum. You're scaring your mother and you're annoying me, so will you please just go back inside and pout there?" I demand. Her eyes narrow and she is silent for a moment.

"Who do you think you are? Ordering *me* around like a child. I will not duck my head and follow your commands. You're not a Commander anymore and I am not one of your soldiers. I highly suggest you turn around and walk away before we have a real problem," she snaps.

"I'm not trying to order you around," I put my hands up again.

"Then go," she crosses her arms.

"I really rather you come with me. We don't know what might happen and you're not in the best condition," I say carefully, watching each and every word to make sure I don't set her off.

"Leave, Maksim. I will come back when I am ready," she sighs, closing her eyes.

"No," I cross my arms, matching her stance. "I'm not too keen on taking orders from you either."

"I'm walking away," she groans and starts to stomp away.

She doesn't get very far before almost tripping and falling. I walk over to her and touch her shoulder. She bats my hand away and tries to keep going. I follow and try to coax her into coming home. She doesn't respond well to my attempts to help her.

"Your mom is probably worried that we aren't back yet. We should really get home," I sigh. She stops dead in her tracks, with her back to me. It's a little frightening; her silence. "I told her I would get you. I'm just trying to help."

"*Home*? What makes you think this is *home*?" her voice is barely a whisper, but thick with anger.

"That's not what I –"

"We were run out of our home!" she turns on me, eyes fiery. "Our home was crawling with murderers! Murderers you called your friends! Murderers like you!" she shouts. "Everything that happened to the Reformation is your fault! Everything that happened to my brother, Mary, Jeremy, and Sonia is *your fault*!"

"If you had any idea how much regret I feel," I shake my head. "I wish you would forgive me, Wren," I admit.

She laughs and tugs at her hair.

"I *have* Maksim! I forgave you before you even asked me to because I know you're better than the awful things you have done! All the harm you have caused," she hugs herself. "I know you're better."

"But you still blame me!" I yell.

"How can I not? If you would have never come into my life, none of this would be happening right now!"

"I told you I won't apologize for that," I blurt out.

"You won't apologize for lying to me?" she hisses.

"I won't apologize for coming into your life. Not everything was a lie. And you know that."

"I forgave you. But I will always blame you. And I'm sorry for that … but it's just how it is," she whispers and lowers her eyes. "I really don't want to do this. I don't understand why you do, but I'm done. I can't handle this right now," she starts to walk away again.

"You're going to make me drag you back. I am not leaving you out here in the middle of the street after a bombing," I growl and continue to follow closely. *Big mistake.*

She turns and swings again, catching me off guard. I barely catch her fist, but she keeps coming at me, just wailing on my chest. She starts to cry as her strikes slow and lose power. She sinks to the ground and sobs, begging me to leave her alone. I can't stand watching her like this, so I reluctantly walk away from her, back to the apartment.

When I walk in, without Wren, Elissa gives me a sympathetic look. I don't explain anything because honestly, I'm not sure I would be able to without losing my composure. I watch from Sonia's window as Wren goes to the graves. She sits in front of Sonia's and Mary's on her knees. Her head is bowed, like she is praying. An hour or too later, she comes back. I hear her close the front door gently before her mom gets to her. I hear both of them sob in the living room until late that night.

When I wake up the next day, Elissa is just getting up from the couch.

"I'm sorry, Vice President Adler, I could have taken the couch," I tell her.

"I'm not the Vice President anymore, Mr. Ozera. And that really isn't necessary. You have given us a place to live in horrible times. You owe us nothing more," she smiles gently. That smile reminds me of my own mother.

"I owe you all more than I care to admit," I scoff and sit on the side chair. There is a heavy silence for a few moments. Her face tells me she knows what I'm thinking. "Where is she?" I whisper.

"In bed. I convinced her to go to the room early in the morning. She is falling apart."

"She just lost two … three, very important people to her."

"One of them being your sister. But here you are. Normal," she smiles again.

"I did my grieving. It's time to move on," I look down.

She stands up and comes over to me, putting her hand on my shoulder.

"That's not how it works … for anyone. Even someone like you," she says softly.

Someone like me …

CHAPTER 8

"Councilman Ozera. There is something we think you should see," a New World Order solider says from the doorway.

The Councilman looks up from his work and sighs.

"Is it urgent?" he asks.

"It's worth your time, sir," the soldier nods.

He leads the Councilman to the video room in Council Headquarters. The Soldier motions to one screen that has footage from the bombing playing on a loop. He tells the man at the computer to rewind to the beginning of the attack. The man does as he is told and lets the video footage play out. As the camera focus' on the rebels on the ground, the Soldier has him pause the footage and zoom in.

Councilman Ozera's blood begins to boil as he stares at the face on the screen. The young man's hair and eyes are much like his own. It's been weeks since he has seen him. He figured the rebels had killed him. He would have never guessed that his own son would have joined them. It was clear he was not being held against his will.

"Put it in slow motion. I want to see what happens," he commands.

The footage begins to play slowly. He sees Maksim run into the hospital and come back out with that rat in his arms and her traitor mother beside him. They are all alive. His jaw starts to hurt from clenching it so hard. The video stops, and he turns his back to the Soldier and the screen.

"Thank you for bringing this to my attention, Soldier," he says before leaving and heading for the President's office. He knocks and enters without permission. His skin is burning his anger. President Zurek looks at him with irritation.

"What do you want?" he growls.

"The rat is still alive. Her mother is alive too. And Maksim ..." he trails off.

The President stands up from his desk and straightens his jacket. "He's alive, isn't he?"

"He's a traitor, Sir. He is with them," Ozera nods.

"Contact his old Commander. Tell him to report here with his best men ASAP," he orders and turns his back to the Councilman, who is about to leave. "Oh, Councilman. One last thing," he looks back at him. "Thank you for your loyalty. I trust that you understand what we must do with your son."

"Of course, Sir. I would do it myself if that were my position."

They must be dealt with. All of them. Even Maksim. He chose this. He chose her.

"If we attack, that means they have home field advantage!" Heath snaps. Jamison sits at the head of the table, rubbing his stubbly chin.

"But if they come here, they will destroy what little we have," I counter. He and I are across from each other. We are Jamison's best men, as he says. He chose us to be his left and right-hand men.

"You shouldn't have a say, you lying bastard!" he leans forward in his seat and grips the table.

I put my hand up defensively.

"Easy, friend. We are on the same side," I say calmly.

Heath is not my biggest fan. He's Wren's oldest brother. I can understand why he isn't fond of me, but for Christ sake, I am doing everything I can to help this damn rebellion, despite everything I ever stood for. And as for Wren, she's better with me. She is able to talk to me without bitterness. That's all this guy should care about, but I guess it doesn't work that way.

"I would rather slit my own throat than trust you with my life, or anyone's here for that matter," he spits. *Dramatic.*

Jamison glare's over at him. "That's enough, Heath," he warns. Heath sits back in his seat and looks over at Alec; Wren's third oldest brother. He shrugs and rolls his eyes, then returns to glaring at me. He's my age. He also does not like me.

It's fine, they're just living in your apartment for a while. No biggie.

"I don't think we should do either," a small voice says from the back of the room, where the lights have burned out. Everyone at the conference table looks back towards the voice. I can't help but smile slightly at the sight of her. "I think we need to go halfway. We find somewhere with cover and protection. We take all units, except one. One stays here as defense in case they get past us," Wren says.

"Wren, what are you doing up?" Jamison sighs and rubs his eyes. He sounds like a dad talking to their toddler late at night. It is late ... and she shouldn't be up. She's been weak lately. Her condition hasn't improved. Elissa thinks that her emotional and mental state is affecting her ability to get better physically. I don't disagree.

"Stopping you guys from making a really dumb decision," she says and comes around to the head of the table and lays out a map. "Here," she points to an abandoned city we passed on our way here on the map. "It has buildings for cover and we can make ourselves familiar with it before they get to us. I doubt they will waste the fuel for another air attack. They'll be on foot next time. And we will be ready."

Everyone at the table nods and there are mumbles of agreement. Jamison looks over his shoulder at her. He smiles and shakes his head in disbelief. She smiles back as she crosses her arms and raises her eyebrows, waiting for his response.

"I think you're right," he nods. "Does anyone disagree or see an issue with this plan?" he asks those at the table. No one replies. "Alright. We leave at noon tomorrow. All units are in, except 5. Unit 5 will be defense. Once you get word that the battle has begun, you get everyone in the bunkers and you do not come out unless we give the okay or we are dead," he orders. Everyone nods promptly and stands up. I stay in my seat, as does Heath. He is staring me down. "It's late, guys."

"Yeah ... we should all get some rest before the walk tomorrow," I mutter and stand up. Heath mirrors me, not taking his eyes off of me.

"Are you going to be able to kill your old buddies, traitor?" he asks me. Jamison glares at him. Wren looks between us, irritated and confused.

"Heath, I no longer have any ties to the N.W.O. I chose this." I tell him. *And your sister.*

"No ties? What about your own father? Or are you going to betray him too? Maybe even kill him yourself? You don't really value family, do you? You were willing to let your sister be executed," he snaps. I reach across the table and grab him by his jacket collar.

"Hey!" a bunch of people shout and are on edge, but no one makes a move.

"My father can burn in hell with the rest of them and I highly suggest you keep my sister out of this unless you want to die," I hiss.

"The rest of them? You *are* one of them!" he grabs my throat and echoes the words I spit at Sonia back home.

"Heath!" Wren screams and grabs his arm, pulling it down. "Maksim!" she turns on me and shoves me back. Her strength takes me by surprise, I almost stumble. "Both of you knock it off! We aren't going to win this war if we start killing each other," she glares at both of us.

"He doesn't belong here," he whispers harshly at her, getting in her face. She gets back in his.

"That's not for you to decide," she whispers back.

"Enough. All of you," Jamison pushes Heath back. "Everyone get out, get back to your homes and go to sleep," he commands. The room starts to empty. Alec doesn't budge from beside Heath. Wren stands with Jamison and I am alone.

"I have proven that I can be trusted," I sigh.

"You've proven nothing to me. You hurt *her.* You put *her* in danger. You almost got *her* killed," he points at Wren.

"I *saved her life*!" I shout.

"Stop!" she yells. "I'm not going to listen to this. We are looking at a war here. Heath, I trust him. Call me stupid or naïve, whatever you want. I trust him. You don't have to. Trust *me*," she begs.

"We have to get home," he mumbles and leaves the room.

We go back to the apartment and then the topic comes up that I think everyone was dreading. Wren wants to come.

"No. Absolutely not," Heath says for the millionth time.

"Wren, you are in no condition to be on a battlefield," Elissa sighs.

"I'm not staying here. No one can make me," she glares at her family. I'm keeping my mouth shut for now. Do I think she should go? No. Hell no. But I have learned there is no winning with her.

"You're being so stupid," Alec grumbles and stands up from the couch. He goes to the kitchen and slams things around.

"You're all being stupid if you think you have any say in what I do and where I go," she hisses.

"I think you should come," I blurt out. Everyone looks at me. No … everyone *glares* at me.

Heath is going to smother you in your sleep.

"You're not a part of this," Elissa says in a warning tone to me.

"She's a big girl," I begin.

"Thank you," Wren pitches in.

"If she wants to get herself killed, let her. It's her choice," I add.

"What?" her eyes narrow.

"Like she said, there's no stopping her," I continue with a shrug.

"I'm not going to get myself killed. I can handle myself," she turns on me.

"I'm not saying you can't. I'm saying you're not in the best condition and it's a bad idea."

She gapes at me. Her eyes burn with anger. If looks could kill … I think I would be dead.

Heath stands up and grabs her shoulders. He turns her towards him.

"Please, Wren. Just use your head," he begs.

"I rather use a gun," she shoves him away and shoots me one last glare before going to *my* bedroom and slamming the door.

I run my hand through my hair and tug it. I should have kept my mouth shut, but she is going to do what she wants. The girl is reckless. Especially lately. She's out for revenge.

"I'm not going in there to get her," Heath says to Elissa. Elissa doesn't seem to want to either. Alec comes out of the kitchen, looking unamused, uninterested and equally unwilling to go in there.

"I'm going to the other room to sleep. You guys have fun fighting her," he mutters and goes to Sonia's room. Alec reminds me of a lost puppy that follows around its owner and does what it is told just to get approval. He barely has a mind of his own.

"Give me a minute," I start heading towards my room. Heath catches me by the arm. It takes everything I have not to swing on him.

"Stay away from her," he snaps.

"You clearly aren't doing any good. Now get your hands off of me or I will break them," I growl.

He lets go and I go to the door. Before I even knock, it swings open. She glares up at me.

"You're one of the most irritating people I have ever met," I tell her. She rolls her eyes and moves to the side, letting me in. After slamming the door and moving to the furthest wall from me, she crosses her arms and meets my eyes.

"I rather be irritating than a liar," she counters.

"Why are you doing this?" I demand. Her jaw drops for a split second, then she clenches it. "You know you aren't in any condition to go."

"What is up with you? A minute ago, you were all for it," she snaps.

"I don't care what you do. I just don't get *why* you are doing this," I reply.

"My brother … is dead. Mary is dead. Jeremy is still missing," she pauses. I can hear the emotion in her voice. I don't like it. "*Sonia* is dead." She continues. I look away from her. "You aren't the only one that feels her loss. She was a real friend of mine. She did something not even you can do," she rambles. I look at her again. "She *always* told me the truth."

"You aren't going to let that go, are you?" I turn away from her and begin to pace. "You can forget all about that ass of a boyfriend *beating* you and now abandoning you, but I lie once for something that I *thought* was right and even apologize *so many* times and you still hold it against me," I spit.

"I was able to get even with Jeremy!" she cries. I look at her. She hugs herself. "I could never lie to you the way you lied to me. I wish I could, Maksim. I wish I could make you feel how I feel every time I look at you!"

"I'm here, now. I've not lied to you since. I gave up everything I had to be here. To save your mom. To save *you*!" I yell.

She flinches.

"That doesn't mean I can trust you! I forgave you. Why isn't that enough?"

I stop and think for a long time. She takes several shaky breaths.

Not the time. You go to war tomorrow. Keep your mouth shut.

"You make me feel things I never felt before. I wish you didn't. But you do. You did from the moment I met you. If I could change history, I would have done things differently. If I would have known how I would end up feeling …" I shake my head. "We need to move past this. This fighting. The bitterness. I have apologized as much as I can handle. I can't stand how you look at me now. You are so cold and … just not you. This isn't you. This isn't the you I was falling –" I stop myself and take a deep breath. "I need to focus on what lies ahead. You need to focus on getting better and then get motivational again. These rebels … they need you. My feelings can't matter right now." I shake my head.

She looks like she is ready to burst into tears because of me…

"I …" she starts. Her hands drop to her sides. "I didn't make you feel anything. I didn't make you lie. I didn't make you do anything you did and for the record, you aren't the only one who feels things. Have you ever thought that being cold was easier than being hurt?" she shakes her head.

No.

"I forgive you, Maksim but I'm not ready to forget. The pain is real. At least for me," she shrugs. I swallow the lump in my throat. "I'm going with the unit's tomorrow. You can tell them that there is no stopping me. Please, get out," she turns her back to me.

I can't make my feet move at first. I stand frozen for a long time.

"Just know … that if something would have happened to you because of me … I wouldn't be able to live with myself."

I finally get out of that room. Heath and Elissa look at me. Their faces are pinched in a way that tells me they heard everything.

"I'll uh … I'll take the couch. Good night."

CHAPTER 9

The walk to the abandoned city takes half the day. We get there by nightfall. I don't talk to my brother's or Mak. I can't even look at Mak. I stay with Jamison towards the back of the army. He tried to tell me that I shouldn't be going. I guess the look on my face was enough to make him give that up. After we get settled in one of the most secure buildings, Heath lights a fire. We all sit around the flames and open our food pouches. The stuff is awful. It was used in the Old World in war. You open the pouch, add some water, stir and enjoy the cold slop. It keeps for a long time though and they are very easy to put together. Mak is on the other side of the fire. His eyes follow my every move. Once I settle across from him, he stands up and makes his way over to my side and sits.

"You looked tired," he says quietly. I nod and stare at the fire. "You should sleep. You need it more than the rest of us," he adds and nudges me. I glare over at him.

"I'm not going to sleep yet," I grumble.

"Alright then," he sighs. "Can I ask you something then?" he asks. I nod. "In the Garden. You knew that hymn better than the rest. Is it your favorite?"

"You could say that," I nod. "My mom used to sing it to my brother's and me when we were younger. She would sing it when we were sad or after dad lost it on one of us. She said it helped the tough times pass," I tell him.

"Did she have to sing it a lot?" he questions.

"Yeah ... I guess. The last time she sang it to me was after I ended things with Jeremy," I smile.

"Was it hard moving on from that?"

"What do you think? You give two years of your life to someone ... and then they turn on you. It hurt for a while. But I got over it and promised myself I would never go back. So, I haven't," I shrug.

"Until he showed up in the bunker."

"Not even then," I glare over at him. "This is bigger him. I didn't have the energy to fight his presence, so I accepted it," I sigh. "We have more important things to worry about, Maksim. We need to stay focused," I look down and leave it at that.

We are here for two days and then we see the N.W.O army making their way towards us. It's time. We have a plan and that's all that we are counting on. We need them to use their ammo before we do. They will have more than us. If we can get them to run low before we start using ours, it gives us a better shot at actually winning this thing.

We are going to have a distraction. We have snipers on the rooftops around us. Me, Jamison, and Wren are going to be unarmed at first and try to get the army in a position where our snipers can easily take out as many as possible. We are going to give them one last chance to negotiate and when they refuse, we run, and pray to God that they miss.

I tried to beg Wren not to be a part of this, but she insisted that seeing her alive would be enough of a distraction to give our people time.

Seeing the number of Soldier's marching towards us actually gives me hope. There aren't as many as I thought there would be. We might have a fair fight. Then I see the tanks behind them. *Shit.*

"We are so screwed," Wren mumbles. She stands between Jamison and me. We have concrete slabs propped up to shield us for when shit hits the fan. Our guns are about five yards back, hidden behind rubble. The rest of our men are hiding in buildings and behind things.

Wren made us several bombs over the past two nights. She was really good at that part of the training at the Academy. Our snipers have them, ready to launch whenever Jamison gives the signal. One should be enough to knock out a substantial portion of these Soldiers. We weren't prepared for tanks though. Who knows? Maybe the bombs will knock those out too. *Probably not.*

"Well. I thought I have seen it all," Commander Jackson steps forward from the army with two other Commanders. He shakes his head at me. "I never would have thought that a Soldier as trained as you would turn against us. All for a rat," he growls.

"Commander Jackson. The weeks have aged you." I grumble. He spits towards us.

"Do you think that helping the weak will get you out of Hell, Ozera? The Lord may forgive, but he doesn't forget. He knows the innocent lives you have taken. He knows the things you have done," he chuckles. The army parts as a tank drives through, stopping behind Jackson and the other two Commanders. "Jamison … The years have not been kind," he purrs. I look over at Jamison, confused. *They know each other?*

"I could say the same for you," Jamison smiles calmly.

My father and Zurek get out of one of the tanks, red hot with anger.

"You son of a bitch," My father hisses. He comes closer to us. Wren clenches her fists. "And you. You're a pest we just can't get rid of," he spits at her.

"We are giving you one last chance to negotiate," Jamison sighs.

"We will not be scared by criminals like yourself," Zurek laughs.

Jamison rubs his chin and lowers his eyes. "Man … that's a shame," he says calmly. "This isn't something we want for anyone. We don't want our people hurt … or any of you."

Get ready.

"We wanted to be a peaceful resistance. We wanted to help you be better. You did this to yourselves. If we can't be peaceful and *smart* about all of this … then I am sorry," he adds and his hand slides to the back of his neck.

Run.

The bomb drops, throwing bodies into the air as it explodes. We run back and duck behind the rubble as we get our guns ready.

Gunfire is going off everywhere. Some is from our snipers, making bullets wiz past our heads. I feel the buzz in my head, right behind my eyes. More bombs drop. Soldiers are yelling and getting behind their tanks. Jamison is shouting into the radios and giving orders. Only the snipers are allowed to fire. Hundreds of bullets are coming our way and being shot into the sky. I put my arms around Wren, covering her head.

One of the tanks fires towards us. It shakes the ground, throwing us around. Jamison gives the order to fire. Everyone. Then it's like Hell on Earth. I prop my gun on the concrete slab and begin to fire shots at anyone in a uniform. I will admit, it feels weird firing at people who used to be friends and teammates of mine. It doesn't stop me.

Wren lays on the ground and fires too. But Jamison … he's on his feet and walking towards them. He uses his gun as a swinging object. It's like he has a shield around him. No bullets are making it to his skin. I am firing at anyone around him. Our people come out of hiding and then real fighting breaks out. Men are tackling each other and going to hand to hand combat.

I spot Commander Jackson making his way towards us. His eyes are on Wren. I jump over the concrete slab and meet him in the middle of it all. He drops his gun and grabs at me. I hit him alongside his head with the butt of the gun until he lets go of my jacket. He drops long enough for me to aim. His eyes meet mine and it's like he knows.

"Do it. Pull the trigger," he grins. I grit my teeth and squeeze the trigger.

After breathing through the nausea that hit me like a brick to the face, I notice that the tanks are left unattended. I call back to Wren and motion towards the one closest to us. She smiles and nods. We bolt towards the tank and our snipers cover us. Wren pulls out a bomb from her bag and lays it underneath the tank.

"How much time do we have?" I yell over the gunfire.

"Not much," she yells back. "Run!"

The bomb goes off, sending the tank flying back. It crushes several Soldiers and the blow sends us flying. It knocks the wind out of me, but when I look over at Wren, her eyes are closed and blood is running from her head, down her cheek.

"Wren?" I shout and crawl towards her.

Bullets fly past our heads. I shake her, but she doesn't respond. I check her pulse. No heartbeat. I drag her to some cover. I just want to yell for everything to stop. It has to stop. How can I help her with a war going on around me?

"Wren … please," I whisper and push the hair from her face. She was already weak. This is all too much. "Shit," I hiss and lay her flat on her back. I shake her harder this time and beg her to wake up.

I need to get her heart beating again. *Now.* I do three chest compressions and then check it again. Nothing. I do more chest compressions followed by mouth-to-mouth resuscitation. I repeat this until another bomb goes off. I stumble and fall to the side of her. She gasps and starts to cough. I grab her shoulders and sit her up.

"Wren?" I gape at her. "Open your eyes. Look at me!" I command.

"Did the bomb work?" she croaks, looking at me with watery eyes. I nod and pull her against my chest, shielding her head as another bomb shakes the ground around us.

"You're an idiot," I mutter into her hair.

Her arms wrap around my torso.

"We need to get out there," she mutters and pushes herself away from me. "We need to finish this," she adds.

I nod and help her stand. "Don't do anything stupid," I tell her as we run towards the action. If I were smarter … I would have made her stay hidden and safe.

CHAPTER 10

Four Weeks Later

It all happened so fast. New World Order planes came in and the ground Soldiers bolted. We didn't know what to do. I remember Maksim yelling for me to run, but I froze. There were no bunkers here. There was nowhere to go. Running ... it was pointless. I remember dropping my gun and watching the planes hover over us. My body was taken out by something other than a bomb. I don't know what that thing was. My head hit the ground pretty hard and I was already weak. Blacking out was a given. I'm not sure if it was Maksim or Jamison. I don't know. Someone took me out and when I woke up ... Heath and Alec were carrying me on a stretcher. They refused to tell me what was going on. All I knew was we weren't going back to the Reformation and we weren't going back to the New World Order Territory.

We met up with Jamison and my mom. Nobody answered my questions for days. When we found a place to be settled along the coast they finally told me everything that happened. I felt ... crushed, to say the least. Everything I had been fighting for was a lie. Everything I thought I knew I could trust ... was gone. Everything I believed in was a lie. And worst of all ... Maksim was taken.

When Jamison started the Reformation in our Territory, he did so because he heard about it in other Territories. The one that we went to when we evacuated was his contact. Their leader, Dominic, was really a New World Order Soldier. It was all a trap. There was no real Reformation anywhere. It was all a ploy to draw out those who wanted to defy the N.W.O. When we went to war, Dominic had planned for his people, who were all loyal to the N.W.O, to contact the main Headquarters and have them send the bombs and then they made it so they would get out in time like the other Soldiers. When they bombed what we thought was the only secure Reformation location, the only people who died were our people. All of us who were at the warzone are physically scarred from the fires that enveloped us.

When the planes came during the war, Maksim is the one who tackled me as the bombs hit. After the planes left, the Soldiers came back. Maksim got me to my brothers in time and stayed to fight off the Soldiers with the rest of the real rebels. I guess that's when he was captured along with others. Peter being one of them.

For some reason, no one thought to help them. I guess everyone panicked. Heath says the smell of burning flesh was so strong, it was nauseating. All of our faces, arms and hands are covered in burns from the bombs. It's a reminder of what they did, and I am thankful for it.

The rest of us came down here. We were fortunate enough that all of Unit 5 were real rebels and they were able to get our people out of the bunkers safely and to the coast with us. We have no guns, no protection, most of our best fighters are dead. If they find us … we are dead. My mother was smart. She brought a radio and all the handheld transceivers she could find.

I always thought they were called "walkie-talkies" because you can walk … and talk. Mak always called them handheld transceivers.

Along the coast, there are small houses with only one or two bedrooms and then one big open area for a kitchen and living room. Mom said that in the Old World, they were used as vacation homes. For the few that made it out, this is home for now. My brother's, mom and I settled in one, but I have been anything but settled. I want answers. I want the whole story.

"Why didn't you get him?" I demand. Heath sighs and looks down.

"Alec and I had you, Wren. We would have been risking your life if we went after him," Heath tells me. He's hiding something. He knows something more. I can see it in his eyes.

"Heath …" I sit on the floor in front of him. He's sitting on the small couch in our living room. Our newest one, that is.

"Look, he's a good guy. He really has your best interest at heart," he shakes his head.

"What happened?"

"Jamison was going to go after him. Maksim told him not to. He told us to go and not come back for him. He begged us, Wren. As they drug him away, all he cared about was that we got you somewhere safe. He didn't want us to help him," he sighs. I stand up and back away.

Why would he do that? He knew what they would do to him once they had him …

"Where did they go?" my father asks for the millionth time. We are on the stage in City Square. My hands are chained to a post and I already have eight lashes on my back.

"For the millionth time … I do not know. We didn't have a plan for running away," I grumble. Another two lashes. Each time, the crowd gasps. I let my head sag and bite tongue hard to keep from screaming. I won't give them the satisfaction.

My father comes around and kneels beside me. He grabs my hair and forces me to look him in the eye. His face disgusts me.

"Just kill me," I growl. My mouth tastes like blood.

"I rather make you suffer," he smiles and drops my head.

Before taking me back to my cell, he whips me five more times. When I am tossed in my cell, the only thing I feel is the blood dripping off my back and down my sides. The lashes burn. I lie there for a long time, not moving. When my cell door opens, I hear clicks of small shoes come closer to me. Probably a nurse. She sits on her knees beside me and pours water on my back. I bite my wrist and groan. Next is alcohol. I swear under my breath. She lays a sheet over my back and then leaves without a word.

When I had realized what was happening during the battle, my only concern was getting Wren out of there. After the bombs stopped dropping, I found Heath and Alec. After they finished demanding to know what I had done to Wren, I handed her over to Heath and told them to get the hell out of there. I wanted to stay and fight the bastards that lied to us.

I was outnumbered and restrained. As they started taking me to a tank to be taken back as a prisoner, Jamison started coming after me.

"Don't!" I shout. Jamison stops and looks confused. "Get out of here! You're going to get yourself killed!"

"Maksim, no!" he shouts back and starts running again.

"Jamison, get *her* out of here! Do not come after me. It's not worth it," I beg. He stops again. He is breathing heavily. "Keep her safe …" I nod as they manhandle me to the tank.

CHAPTER 11

The nightmares don't stop. All I see is what they did to me when I was a prisoner … but it's Maksim now. Every night I wake up at least once, screaming or crying. Mom has stopped trying to console me. Instead she just goes to the living room until I stop. Then she'll come back in and lie down again to go to sleep.

So many people are dead. Everything changed so quickly. It's almost March now. This all started in December, when Mak followed me to the lookout tower. I can't even say that I wish I never met him … because I don't wish that at all. I just wish it would have been under different circumstances. I know that what I felt was real … and I know he felt it too. It was all real. Call it what you want. I just have to go back for him. He would do it for me.

I sit up, gasping. Tears soak my cheeks and my pillow. My mother stirs beside me and starts to get up to go to the couch. I touch her shoulder and gently push her back down. She groggily thanks me before going back to sleep.

I slip out of the bed and slip on my shoes and jacket. I go outside and walk off the wooden porch and into the sand. It's almost sunrise. I walk along the beach until I get to Jamison's hut. I knock lightly, not wanting to wake him if by chance he is sleeping. The door swings open and he smiles at me.

"Did I wake you?" I ask him. He holds up a bottle of whisky and shrugs. "Can I join you?" I smile. He nods and lets me in.

We sit in his living room and drink until the sun is above the horizon. We don't speak for a long time. He's not yet been able to properly grieve Mary. No one has had time to grieve. I look over at him.

"What are we going to do, Jamison? What do we have left?" I whimper.

"We all have each other. We have the Reformation."

"The Reformation was a lie," I snap at him.

"No, it wasn't," he snaps back. "Not to us," he adds.

"It's gone now. We don't have any supplies. We are officially screwed," I grumble and take another swig of whisky. It's disgusting by the way and I have no idea where Jamison got it. But hey, whatever does the trick right?

"We need to get our people back," he nods confidently, as if it is just that easy.

"Yeah. Easier said than done," I snort.

"Nothing has been easy for us," he looks over at me and takes his whisky. He finishes it off and stands up, groaning. I watch him carefully. "I'm gonna go get 'em," he slurs.

"Not right now," I sigh and follow him. I grab his shoulders and turn him away from the front door. I lead him to his bedroom. "Lie down," I command. He falls back and drops the bottle on the floor. I kick it under the bed. "Once you're rested and sober, we will go," I tell him. He nods and flops over on his stomach, groaning. He'll probably puke soon. I feel like I might.

I go out to the beach and walk down to the water. Nausea hits me like wave. I throw up in the ocean. As I do, a literal wave comes up and knocks me back into the water. Vomit is down the front of my shirt and now I am wet, cold and have sand all over me. I swear under my breath and go back to the house. Heath and Alec give me looks when I walk in the door but know better than to say anything.

I take a long shower and when I get out, I stare at myself in the mirror. I don't look like I used to. Scars from torture and fire cover my skin. My eyes have dark circles around them and my cheeks are sunken in. You can still see my ribs from when I was starved in the prison. And there is a scar from where I was shot. I look like a ghost of who I used to be.

I shake my head, disgusted, and wrap a towel around myself. I go to the bedroom and grab a pair of faded jeans with the least number of holes and stains. The long sleeve I grab is Maksim's. I pull it on and push my feet into my boots.

My mom stops me as I pass through the kitchen. She makes me sit and eat, just like old times. Heath and Alec join me. Both are awkwardly silent. I look between them while we eat. They won't make eye contact. When I look at mom, she won't either.

"What's up with you people?" I demand. Alec looks down, my mother turns around and busies herself with cleaning dishes, and Heath glances at me. "You're all acting sketchy," I hiss.

"We are just worried about you," Alec shrugs.

"Bull. What's going on?" I growl.

"You can't get mad. This is the best option we have," Heath sighs. I glare over at him. "While you were off drinking with Jamison, mom and some of the others were able to contact the Free World," he tells me.

"The Free World? How did you ..." I shake my head.

"My job as Vice President of the Council of the New World Order was to make sure that we stayed civil with our trading partners. The Free World is one of those partners. With the radio ... I was able to contact them and explained the situation. They had already heard about it and said they would be willing to send help to get us," my mother explains.

"Get us? As in come get us and then help us get our people back?" I ask. Heath and Alec exchange looks. "We are going to get our people back right? We are going to get Maksim. We aren't just going to leave them ..." I trail off.

"As of right now ... we do not have plans for a rescue," she answers.

"You're kidding," I stand up and back away. "We are just going to leave all of them?" I cry.

"We don't have the means necessary to help them right now," Heath says.

"They would come for us. Maksim would come for us," I shake my head. I feel my heart starting to race with panic. We can't just leave them. We can't.

"Maksim would come for *you*," mom sighs.

Tears trickle down my face. "And that means I need to go for him! That's how it works!"

"We will come back for them when we have the full support of the Free World," she reaches for me. I back away more.

"They won't help us. They refuse to fight! They refuse to stand up against the New World Order as long as they are civil!" I yell. They all flinch. I storm out of the house and down to the water.

My hands and knees shake. If we leave them, we are just as bad as the N.W.O. Maksim did what he had to, to make sure I was safe. I owe him. There is no way my brothers are going to let me stay here. They will drag me, kicking and screaming before they leave me here.

The Free World is far North. We would have to pass by the Territory to even get to the Freeland. It would be no inconvenience to just stop in and get our people back. I guess it doesn't work that way though. If the Free World is caught helping rebels, that means the peace agreement is off between them and the N.W.O. Jamison and I can't go alone either. There really are no other options right now.

The door creaks open and Soldiers come in to take me to the room. They have tried every torture technique they can think of. I don't have any finger or toe nails left. I have been choked, beaten, starved, tortured every way possible. They have an electric chair now. My skin has been branded with iron rods. If I am being completely honest, I don't know if I would have been able to keep their location secret if I knew it. That's the worst part. They really think I know something, and I just don't.

They take me into the room and tie me to the chair like they do every day. My father comes into the room with another man. The man is carrying a small briefcase. I've seen the man in passing before, but never thought twice about him. Now, seeing him here, I have a pretty good idea what he does.

"Maksim say hello to Ruslan Kal. He's going to be working with you for a few hours today," my father says with a wicked grin on his face. I say nothing.

"I'm sure you've seen me before, am I right?" Kal asks. I glance over at him and then look away. "I work in Specialty Information's. Do you know what that means?"

"You torture people to get information," I grumble.

"Basically, yes. I've been told I am very good at my job," he smiles. *Congrats.*

"Maksim was good at his job once," my father mutters. I smile at the ceiling.

"I want to give you a chance to tell me what you know," Kal tells me.

I lift my head and resist the urge to scream.

"I've told everyone for *weeks* that I don't know anything! The rebels didn't have a backup plan if the battle went poorly! If they aren't in the south city, then I don't have a clue where they went!" I snap.

"We'll see about that," Kal sighs and opens his briefcase on the table beside the chair. I look at the various torture tools and then at my father.

"You're out of your mind! I don't know anything! I would have told you by now!" I shout.

"You chose this when you chose the girl," he shrugs.

"It's bigger than that! Don't you see that? What they stand for … it's right!" I ramble, but it's no use. My father leaves the room and the torture begins.

The human brain can only stay sane for so long when it endures pain for an extended period of time. Eventually, you snap. I think it's safe to say that Ruslan Kal made me really snap.

CHAPTER 12

"I have done everything. He insists he doesn't know anything about the rebels. I think it's time we believe him and make another move because the boy has lost it. He broke. There is nothing we can get from him that will be of use," Kal tells his audience which a blend of Commanders, Soldiers, Councilmen and President Zurek.

"If he doesn't know anything … then we lie. We break him more. Not just physically or mentally. We've done that quite well." Zurek chuckles. He looks around the room, meeting the eager eyes of his sheep. "We tell him the girl is dead. We tell him that our Soldiers found them and killed them. Give him details if that's what it takes to break his last source of motivation," he tells them. When he sees smiles spreading across their faces, he feels content, at least for the moment.

The hummers pull up out of nowhere. Everyone has their things packed already and start to move towards the vehicles. I sit with my bag on the front porch of our little hut and watch the waves. My mom and brothers gather the last of their things and take them to one of the hummers. I don't budge. I still have on Mak's sweater. The Free World Soldiers arrived earlier than expected, but everyone was waiting, ecstatic. Everyone but me and Jamison.

My mother finally comes and gets me, grabbing my bag with one hand and grabbing my arm with her other hand. She pulls me behind her to the hummer. I jerk away from her grasp and walk ahead of her. I get in the back with my brothers and she gets in the passenger seat. The Soldier driving tells us to buckle up and then pulls out onto the road.

Here we go.

When we get to the Free World, after a long drive, we are all taken to the Free World Council building. It's light and clean. There are pictures of the community doing services with President Amendola around the Territory. The Free World doesn't have Soldier's like the New World Order. But there is Security. They stop us in a big waiting room.

"Which one of you contacted President Amendola?" a man asks. My mom steps forward. "Come with us," he turns on his heel and starts to walk away. My mom looks back at me and motions for me to follow. I nudge Jamison and the three of us follow the Security man.

We are led into a plush office. The man opens the door for us and motions us in. There is a woman sitting behind the desk. I can only imagine she is Isabelle Amendola. Her honey blonde hair is pulled into a low, neat bun and her olive skin is flawless. She painted her lips red and shaped them into a smile as soon as we walked in. It's the kind of smile that doesn't reach her eyes.

"Welcome. It is so nice to have you here. Who is Elissa Adler?" President Amendola asks.

"Me, Ma'am. But I'm not the one who needs to speak with you. My daughter, Wren ... she's kind of in charge here," my mom smiles at me. She says that like it's a good thing.

"Wren Adler. You have gotten yourself in quite the predicament," Amendola chuckles.

"I'm not here to entertain friendly banter, especially not about what we have been through," I hiss. She lifts her chin and her smile fades. "The New World Order has men and women that fought for a cause I convinced them was worth dying for. A lot of people did die. Those that didn't either escaped or were captured by the N.W.O and are being tortured as we speak. I will not stay here unless I know you will help me get them back," I tell her. She raises her eyebrows and looks past me at my mother and Jamison. I cross my arms and stand firm.

"And who might you be, sir?" she asks Jamison.

"Jamison Richards. I'm with her," he answers and grabs my shoulder.

"Right ... well I don't know what to tell you, Ms. Adler. We are currently at peace with the New World Order Territories and even having you here puts us at risk of losing that peace. That's not something I want for my people. We are peace loving people," she smiles softly.

"The people of the Reformation were peace loving people ... until we couldn't be anymore," I growl and step closer to her desk. "Sometimes turning the other cheek doesn't do the trick."

"I understand that you are upset, Ms. Adler –"

"You understand nothing!" I yell. "You sit here in your cozy office and, and you go home to your cozy house while your citizens go to their normal jobs and their kids go to school to learn about poetry and how to add. Meanwhile ... there are innocent people dying for breathing the wrong way in the New World Order," I spit.

"Enough," she snaps and stands. "I will talk to some people. I make some arrangements for you and your friends. If there are any volunteers to go with you, I can't stop them. But I will not force anyone to do anything. Especially if it means getting killed," she sighs. "Now ... if you're done," she mutters.

"For now," I reply.

"There are some apartments on the East side of the city for you and your friends," she tells me.

"That is greatly appreciated, President Amendola," My mom speaks up.

"You should all go ... get settled in and rest up. You've had a long journey," she dismisses us. I turn without another word.

I go and relay the message to the others. We move in a group to the building. After a lot of convincing, my mother agrees to let me stay alone. When I get to my apartment, I lock the door and go to the bathroom. I lock that door too and turn the shower on. I bite down on my sleeve and let out a scream. My stomach twists in knots. These people are cowards. Selfish cowards. They are willing to let our people die because they are afraid of what might happen. They have their money and their perfect lives here. Nothing else matters.

After I get everything out of my system, I get in the shower. The soaps here smell like flowers and vanilla. They are colorful and some shimmer. We don't have anything like this back home. I guess I shouldn't call it home anymore.

When I get out, I get dressed in the pajamas they gave me. I pull on the black pajama bottoms that are silky and a baby blue long sleeve silky top. I like the silk material because it doesn't hurt as much when it rubs against my burns.

Before I get to my bedroom, there is a knock on my door. I look through the peephole.

"President Amendola, what a lovely surprise," I lie as I open the door. She smiles at me.

"May I come in?" she asks. I nod and step to the side. "You are very spirited, Wren Adler," she chuckles and sits down on the couch.

I sit in the chair cross from her.

"Ma'am, I am sorry if I stepped out of line earlier. You just don't understand," I tell her.

"You're right. I have not seen what you have seen. I have not endured what you have. I can't imagine what you are feeling," she shakes her head. "But you need to see my side," she says firmly. "It is my duty to protect my people. This Domain is built on peace and trust. It would be foolish for me to put my people in danger. They outnumber and outweigh those taken by the New World Order. I hope you can understand that," she says.

"I can. But that doesn't mean I am going to give up," I snap.

She smiles again.

"Like I said, you are very spirited. That's why I am here. I am unwilling to put my people in danger. I am unwilling to put my Domain in danger. But I am willing to make a deal with you. That way we can both get what we want," she leans back and crosses her legs. "Is that something you would be interested in?" she asks.

"It depends," I growl.

She laughs dryly.

"I will help you get your people back and take down the N.W.O," she says. My heart skips. "But it will be done without violence and I want you to be the leader of the Rising," she smiles.

"The what?"

"The Rising. A way to take the New World Order down," she answers.

"What would I have to do?" I question.

"Meet with my security and formulate plans. Execute missions," she shrugs as if it's nothing.

"And if I agree to be the lead of this, you will give me the supplies and power I need to get my people back?"

"It will be your very first mission," she nods.

"Fine. When do I start?" I stand up. She mirrors me.

"Come to my office tomorrow, dressed appropriately, and we will get started."

"See you in the morning," I murmur as I open the door. She leaves, giving me one last fake smile before I close and lock the door.

"Wren, this is Ivan Brookes," Amendola introduces me to a man in his early thirties. His deep brown hair is a lot like Mak's …

"Hi Wren. You can call me Brookes. Everyone else does. I'm kind of like a journalist. I'm covering this story. It's very nice to meet –"

"Why is he here?" I hiss.

"I want this to be a moment remembered all throughout history," she frowns.

"Fine. Stay out of my way," I grumble and brush past him.

"Wren, your hair," she chases after me. I keep walking towards the conference room where my first meeting will be. Amendola provided me with some of the best Security members she has. I just have to convince them to join me and then make the first rescue plan. The rest of my fellow rebels are already waiting for me. "Ms. Adler, please."

"I have more important things to worry about than my hair, Ma'am. Now please, let me do what you have asked me to do," I snap. She nods and walks away from me as I enter the room.

Almost two dozen faces look back at me. Many looked surprised to see that their potential leader is a little girl. I adjust my button up shirt and sit down at the head of the table.

"I want to start by thanking everyone for coming," I clear my throat. "I know that things are very different here. I could never expect anyone to understand what I grew up with. Asking you to join me in taking the New World Order down is a lot. It's dangerous and it will not be easy. There are some people being tortured right now because they thought this was a cause worth fighting for and they did fight. After losing countless loved ones and friends, they still fought. The Old World wasn't perfect. But there weren't mass executions and bombings on your own people. There weren't murderers in power. There was still beauty and moments of humanity. For those who live under the New World Order's thumb, there is none of that. There is no sign of hope. I'm begging you ... look into your hearts. If these people were your friends and family ... wouldn't you want someone to go after them?"

Blank faces stare back at me. My fellow rebels keep their eyes on me, hoping for some sort of relief, but there is nothing. I stand up and do my best to keep my composure. Their eyes follow my every move, making it even more frustrating.

"I understand this is a lot to consider. I don't want to force anyone into doing this. I'll give you the day to consider. Tomorrow ... if you're with me, meet me back here at noon. We can go from there. Thank you for your time," I nod before leaving the room.

All we can do is wait ...

CHAPTER 13

When I had come back the next day, almost all of the men and women that sat before me the day prior had returned. They were ready to fight with me against the New World Order, but before anything else, we needed to get the other rebels back. We needed to get Maksim back. Planning began and it was long and hard. There were too many debates to keep track of. I faced questions as to why these people were so important and why we couldn't just get them after taking the New World Order down. Thank God for Jamison and my brother's being there.

The day is approaching. I am terrified. We could get there and find that all of our friends and family dead. We could get caught and then it's all over. Then it was all for nothing. I can't let my fear get in my way. We have our goal and we have the numbers and the power to reach it. We just need to do it.

"We need offense and defense. We need people on the outside, ready to help us get the hell out of there," Heath snaps.

"We can't leave anyone on the outside. We need to stick together or else we will have another rescue mission to plan," Jamison snaps back. All of us are sitting in a conference room getting ready for tomorrows mission. I rub my eyes and lean back in my seat. "You know I'm right, Wren," he adds.

"No splitting up. We are a team. We stick together, and we get our people out. We don't leave anyone behind," I tell them and stand up. "We will leave tomorrow morning. Make sure the cars are gassed up beforehand. We won't be stopping," I tell them and start to leave the room.

Before leaving, I thank everyone again and tell them to get rested for tomorrow. It's going to be a long, horrible day. Many people shake my hand and hug me, occasionally kissing my cheek. Some even thank me, but I should be thanking them. Not the other way around.

When I get back to my apartment, I go to the bathroom and wipe off the layers of makeup from my face. I turn on the shower and let it warm up enough to where there is steam on the mirror, then I get in. I stand there, hugging myself and letting the hot water turn my pale skin pink. I scrub my scalp with the fruity shampoo and lather my skin with the floral body wash. After I rinse everything away, I force myself to get out and wrap a big towel around myself.

My body is heavy as I carry it to the bedroom. I don't have the energy to get dressed. I lay down in bed and pull the sheets over myself. I don't even turn out the lights. Surprisingly, sleep comes easily. My eyelids get heavy and then there is just nothing, but I am strangely aware of how long I am asleep.

When my alarm goes off at 7 a.m. I groan.

I sit up and adjust the towel around me. I go to the closet and look at my best options for a rescue mission. After settling on black jeans and a black sweater that is a little too big for me, I get dressed and find my old boots. I pull my hair back into some sort of knot. It feels really nice to walk out of the apartment without makeup for the first time in the few weeks we have been here.

It took a long time to get this mission officially approved and planned out, with backup plans and last-minute changes. Us rebels had to teach the others how to shoot a gun the right way. I guess they never had to before. They carried, but never had to fire. How lucky they are.

When I get to the Council building, everyone is gathered in the lobby, waiting. There is about forty of us all together and we are missing about ten of my rebels. We have minimal weapons. It's going to take some badass trickery to get into the prison and out with everyone.

The cars are outside, gassed and ready to go. I grab a gun from the table and sling it over my shoulder, then turn to the faces that stare back at me, waiting. Many eyes are full of fear. Some with anger. Few with hope.

"It's a scary thing to walk into something that could be considered a death mission. For most of you … it's for people that you don't even know. I can never thank you enough. We are at war … and that's just a fact now. I promise you … without these people, it's not a war we will be able to win. But there is hope. We are getting them back today. No one will be left behind. Dead or alive … everyone will be coming back to the Freeland to either celebrate … or to be memorialized. Be alert and don't be afraid to pull the trigger if you have to," I tell them. Everyone nods and there is a buzz in the air. "Let's load up!" I yell and go to the first car. Jamison gets in the driver's seat and my brothers get in the back. I get in the passenger seat and once all the cars are loaded up, we leave.

The drive is a blur. It takes all day and into the night to get there. We knew it would. I run every scenario through my head until we arrive. Some don't play out well. The Territory is dark when we arrive. Not a light shines in the windows of the buildings. When we get to the edge of town, it's clear that it's gone downhill. Trash is everywhere. There is the smell of death everywhere. They've been killing a lot of people … it's like a ghost town.

We use the sewers to get into the city. Jamison used to work for the city. He knew everything there was to know about it and its layout. He even knew of a secret entrance to all the basements of most buildings, including the prison. We stop at the entrance and everyone huddles close together.

"I'm going in. I will give the all clear," I tell as quietly as possible. Heath grabs my arm and shakes his head no.

"Let me," he says.

"Get your hand off of me and get in position," I hiss and jerk away from him.

I've been getting really sick of being treated like a paper doll. Underdog. Damaged. It's all what other people want me to be. I refuse. I am a survivor. I have been trained to fight and kill. God did not put me on this planet to be the underdog. He did not put me here to be damaged. I was never meant to be soft and quiet. I am meant to stand my ground and the ground of those who cannot stand on their own. I am meant to make my enemies shake when they hear my name. I'm not the little girl I once was. I am a woman, shaped and carved by pain and loss. I will not sit back and let anyone else do what needs done.

I tiptoe in, which is almost pointless because the door was louder than a sneeze during prayer in church. Everything is dark and damp. I remember this place from my memorable time here. I am at the back of the prison. I can see the glow of the office light where the guard is on watch. Hopefully it's only one. I look in the cells as I pass by. I see our people passed out on the cold cement floor. When I get up to the office, I stop before the door. In the cell across from the office, I see Maksim with his arms chained above his head, which is sagging. Even in the dark, I can see his jawline, which is covered in bruises.

The guard is passed out in his chair. I quietly lay my gun down outside of the office and walk on my toes into the office. There are computer screens with security footage of the whole prison. He's the only guard here right now and he's probably supposed to be doing rounds. Luckily for us ... he's not. I stand behind him and take slow breaths before wrapping my right arm around his fat neck and pulling it tight with my left arm. He jumps up, almost throwing me off. He swears and starts to grab at me, so I squeeze harder. He backs into the cinderblock wall, squishing my body. I force my feet up to his back and push his body away from mine, while still squeezing his neck as hard as I can.

He gasps for a long time before finally falling. I clumsily get to my feet and quickly handcuff him with his own cuffs. I don't bother checking his pulse. I only check the cameras one last time, grab the cell keys and then leave the office, closing the door.

As I run back to the door to give the all clear, I see a lot of the rebels are up now and their tired eyes fill with hope. I pop my head through the door and smile at the team. They all smile back and cheer quietly as they swarm in and start unlocking the doors. Jamison and I run back down to the end where Maksim's cell is. His eyes are open now and he is looking at us, but I don't think he is seeing us. Jamison opens the door and I run in, falling to my knees beside him.

"Mak?" I whimper. He looks at me carefully. His eyes are bloodshot and sunken in. He's lost some weight. Any muscle he had is probably gone. "Maksim, you're okay now," I touch his bruised face.

"You're not really here," he mutters like a zombie. "You can't be," his voice is hoarse.

"Of course, I'm here ... I'm standing right in front of you," I tell him as Jamison gets his hands lowered. Mak shakes his head and his eyes begin to water.

"This has to be a dream … this can't be real," he trembles.

"Come on, buddy," Jamison starts to pick him up and he freaks out.

"Get your hands off of me!" he shouts and elbows Jamison in the face, making his nose bleed. I reach for Maksim and touch his face, begging him to look at me, telling him I'm real and I'm really there. He grabs my wrists and shoves me into the wall. I hit my head hard. "Haven't you done enough?! You killed her! You killed her and now you mock me!" he yells, slamming my body against the wall harder. Jamison comes up behind him and hits him with his gun.

Maksim crumbles to the ground, passed out. I fall beside him, on the verge of tears. What have they done to him?

"We have to get out of here," Jamison says and pulls Mak up. I nod and help him. We get out of the cell and head for the door with the others. No one else seems to be freaking out. No doubt they were the hardest on Mak.

We are almost to the edge of town again, when we hear shouting behind us. We look back and see New World Order Soldiers running in the dark behind us. Everyone swears.

"Guns!" I shout. Everyone with a gun comes forward. Jamison and I hand Mak over to Peter and another rebel. There are bullets flying. I turn back to those who didn't have guns and those we rescued. "Get back to the cars and wait for us! Go! Now!" I order. They start to flee for the ladder to the surface where our cars are. I pray Soldiers aren't there waiting for them.

"We have to get out of here, Wren!" Heath shouts. I look over at him and Alec.

"Go with the others. There might be Soldiers waiting for them," I tell them.

"Are you crazy? Not without you!" he snaps.

"Please!" I beg. "I'll be there soon. We all will. Go!" I push him away and go back to shooting. Some of the Soldiers are dropping, which means we are hitting our targets. The others realize that and press themselves against the wall for cover. "Start backing up," I command those who are left.

We inch our way back and they inch forward. When we get to the ladder, I go nuts. Some might call it trigger happy. Team members start to climb the ladder. Jamison and I are the last two. We climb and shoot until its safe enough to make a break for it. We see the cars with our people in them, ready to make a break for it.

"Run!" Jamison shouts.

We go, and the Soldiers follow. Occasionally I'll turn and shoot at the few left. Once Jamison and I get into our car where Heath and Alec are in the front and Mak is slouched in the back seat, we go. Bullets break through many windows but our whole team is there and driving away from the N.W.O. Over the radios, everyone is celebrating.

"Is everyone okay? Do we have everyone?" I ask over the radio. I get several confirmations and then the celebrating continues. "I'll see everyone back home," I sigh and turn off my radio.

I'm in between Mak and Jamison. Heath is booking it and everyone else seems to be keeping up, so I let my head fall back against the seat. I look over at Mak. In the light of the moon I can see that he doesn't have any finger nails left and he is covered in his own blood. There are marks in his arms from needles it looks like. What did they do to him?

I watch him, the whole drive back to the Freeland. I don't sleep, as much as I want to. I stare at him. I watch his eyelids as they occasionally twitch. I watch his chest rise and fall as he breathes. A part of me wants him to wake up and talk to me. Most of me is scared of him waking up. He looked at me with such hatred in that cell. He's completely lost it …

CHAPTER 14

We got back to the Freeland around dawn. All of the prisoners were taken to the Medical Center where they were immediately treated and taken care of. Maksim was strapped to the gurney as soon as he was put down. I watched them wheel him away. The doctors told me to go home to get some sleep and come back later. They said it might take a little while to do what they had to do.

I wake up, still in the jeans and sweater. My hair is in a big knot on top of my head and my face looks awful. I feel a bump on the back of my head from hitting it so hard. My wrists are bruised. I sit up in bed and let myself adjust to the late afternoon sun, shining in the window. I shove my feet back into my boots and leave the apartment. I see my brothers and mother in the lobby of the apartment building. My mom hugs me looks me up and down. After telling me how worried she was she hugged me again.

"I should go see if Mak is awake. He'll need me," I mutter.

"Be careful … I saw what he did to you," Heath growls.

I glare over at him.

"He didn't know what he was doing," I shake my head and walk past him.

People gawk at the mess I am as I walk to the hospital. The woman at the front desk sees me coming and points to the elevators. She tells me he's on floor 3, room 24. I nod and take the stairs two at a time up to the third floor. I go to his room and see him lying in the bed asleep. There is a doctor checking on him. I knock lightly and step in.

"You must be Wren," she smiles at me. I nod. "We've had an IV going for hours. He's severely dehydrated and malnourished. We had to rebreak a few ribs to reset them and his nails are gone. All of them. They need to stay wrapped until they start to heal. We are all surprised he's even alive right now. We've never seen trauma this severe in someone still breathing," she tells me.

"Is he going to be okay?" I ask.

"The physical trauma will heal with time. He'll need to be on bed rest for a while, but we think with the proper care …" she pauses and smiles slightly at me. "He will recover just fine. It's his psychological state that we might have to be worried about. You need to let us know immediately if he shows any of these warning signs. Being tortured for two months does more damage than physical," she says, handing me a piece of paper with the warning signs listed.

Trust me, I know.

"When will he be awake?" I glance up at her.

"Whenever his body is ready," She touches my shoulder and leaves.

I sit in the hard chair beside his bed for hours. I can only look at him for so long before having to look out the window instead. Nurses come in and check his blood pressure and heart rate every hour. Close to sunset, he groans and begins to stir. I stand up and watch him. His eyes open slowly and immediately begin to scan the room. When he looks at me, they begin to water again.

"Wren?" he asks. I nod and swallow the lump in my throat. "I thought you were dead. They said … they said they killed you," he mutters, shaking his head in disbelief.

"I'm very much alive," I force a smile.

"What happened? Why am I strapped down?" he questions.

"We are in the Freeland. I made a rescue team. We came and got everyone out … we got you out," I reassure him. He looks down at the restraints. "And uh … and your mind was messed up. You freaked out on me and Jamison," I add and look down. He lets his head fall back and he thinks for a long time. I want to tell him he's okay now.

"I hurt you," he mumbles. "I remember …" he trails off.

"You didn't know what you were doing," I shake my head. He closes his eyes tight. "We are both okay. You are okay now," I reach for his hand. He tries to move it away, but the restraint stops him. I let my hand fall to my side. "Here …" I whisper. I undo the straps on both sides and then his ankles.

He watches me sadly.

"You should leave," he says.

I stop and force myself to look him in the eye.

"What?" I ask.

"I've hurt you too many times," he growls.

I grab his hand.

"I'm not playing this game with you, Maksim. We have done too much for each other. I didn't put these people's lives in danger to get you back ... just for you to push me away. Everything that happened before ... the lies and the betrayal, it's all over," I hiss. He won't look at me. "Mak, we are officially past that. You made it up to me, okay? You made us even," I insist.

"But I hurt you ... after saying I would never hurt you again," he shakes his head and looks up at me. "They said they tracked down the rebels that escaped from the battle. They told me once they found you ... they killed your brothers, making you watch. They said when you were the last one left ... they killed you slowly. Beating you ... breaking you until there was nothing left to break ... and then they shot you," he tells me.

"They lied, Mak. To hurt you. They were doing everything they could to break you down until there was nothing ... and I think it worked. That wasn't you back there. You lost it."

"I have to get better before they attack. You know they are going to. If the Free World helped you conduct a rescue mission, the New World Order is going to burn the Peace Treaty," he says and winces as he tries to sit up.

"Oh, after what we did ... they are going to do more than that," Jamison muses from the doorway. I smile at him as he walks in and grabs the television remote. He turns it onto the news. A Free World reporter is sitting behind the desk on the screen going over the events of the rescue mission for the nightly news. He turns up the volume.

"Wren Adler was the leader of this mission and seems to have become the accidental face of the Free World's rise against the New World Order," the reporter says. A picture of me pops up on the screen beside the reporter's head. "People are wondering if this means war. We now go to the Council for answers."

The screen switches to a conference room in the Council Building. Isabelle stands behind a podium with a microphone and cameras flash and people raise their hands to ask questions.

"President Amendola! Are we going to war with the New World Order? Who is going to protect us?" someone demands.

"We have our own security team that is trained just as well as the Soldiers of the New World Order. With the help of Wren Adler and her team of rebels, we will rise against the New World Order and create a Free World for all."

Jamison turns off the TV and looks back at us.

"She's signing the rebels up for war," Maksim murmurs.

"She is signing everyone up for war. We don't have a choice now. After we did what we did … that's all that is left to do," I shrug.

"I need to get out of here," Maksim tries to get out of the bed and sucks in a breath, gripping his side. I put my hand on his shoulder and lightly push him back down.

"You're aren't walking out of this hospital tonight, Mak. Not for a while," I tell him.

"I don't want to be in here," he argues.

"One week … I'll check you out in one week," I sigh. "And you can come stay with me," I add.

"Are you sure about that, Wren? He's going to need constant care for a while," Jamison says.

"I know," I look at him and nod. I look back down at Maksim. His eyes search my face. Jamison sighs and leaves. "I'll be back tomorrow. I'll stay with you during the days until you can walk out of here," I reassure him.

"To a tiny apartment with your mom and brothers?" he scoffs.

"No. To an apartment that I stay in all by myself," I counter. "Thanks to the *generosity* of President Isabelle Amendola, all the rebels that weren't captured were provided with their own apartments and some have even started work here. They've started new lives."

"Generosity to use against you if you step out of line," he mumbles and looks away from me.

"I've done my part and it's over now. I got you out of there," I nudge him.

"No … you're the leader of the rising. You're the face. It's not over yet. That would be too easy," he says quietly, almost to himself.

"I need your help with this, Mak," I whimper. He looks over at me. "I only got roped into this gig because I needed to get you back. Because you would have done it for me. You *have* done it for me. Now that you're here, I need you to be by my side … to keep me from doing something stupid."

My eyes fill with tears. I blink them away and swallow the growing lump in my throat. He squeezes my hand and nods. When I leave, Jamison is waiting to walk me back to the apartment. We don't say much but I know he doesn't like the idea of me taking care of Maksim. I don't blame him … but as much as I hate to admit it, I need Maksim. I need his mind. Even in this state, I'm sure he has more clarity than me.

I spend my days in the hospital, in a chair beside Mak's bed. He sleeps often, but even when he is awake, he says little. I don't push him to tell me what happened to him in the prison, because on the rare occasion he feels like talking about it, I feel sick hearing about it. My brother's and mom come to visit once or twice. Mom does most of the talking each time, while Heath and Alec stand close to the door with their hands in their pockets. Maksim thanks them for coming with me to get him out of there. To no surprise, Heath reminds him it wasn't just for him. After a week, Maksim starts asking when he can leave.

"Tomorrow … I'll take you home tomorrow," I give in.

"Home," He scoffs. It reminds me of the fight we had in the South City. "This isn't home."

"It's close enough for now. I'll see you in the morning. Get some sleep," I tell him before leaving.

The next morning, I am summoned to President Amendola's office. I make my way across the city and once I am there, I find her waiting for me in the lobby of the Council Building. She stands and comes to greet me with a big smile and open arms. I wait for her to make a comment about my hair or lack of makeup and less than best clothes, but it never comes.

"Congratulations on a successful rescue mission," she says once we get to her office.

"Thank you," I force a smile. "It's time to start planning our next move, I assume."

"With time," she waves her hand dismissively. "This conversation can be quick. I know you have to get to the hospital to be with Maksim Ozera … but there are just a few loose ends to tie up," she smiles briefly and pulls out a pile of paperwork.

"For what?" I ask.

She wiggles her arched eyebrows at me. "To officially register you as a Free World Protector." The morning is filled with signing papers and reading contracts. By the time we are done, it's past noon. I anxiously wait to be dismissed.

"I will send a car with you to get your friend. We have some extra apartments. I will get one ready for him –"

"That's not necessary," I cut her off. "He's going to be staying with me," I tell her. "He needs taken care of still."

"I see …" she nods and the corner of her mouth twitches ever so slightly. She doesn't like being turned down on an offer. "Well then I will send a car anyway … that way he doesn't have to walk all that distance. I'll also arrange for some clothes to be delivered," she says and calls her driver.

He meets me out front and takes me to the hospital. I tell him just to wait out front while I go to get Maksim. When I get to his room, he is sitting up, getting his torso wrapped by a pretty blonde nurse. I've seen her a few times when I was here. I stop in the doorway and watch as she takes her time and occasionally touches his arm and apologizes for making him wince. I cross my arms uncomfortably. When he opens his eyes and sees me, he lets out a sigh of relief.

"It's about damn time you got here," he grumbles. The nurse looks back at me and her expression turns to surprise when she recognizes me as the rebel girl that's been at his side for days.

"I got caught up with some things. I'll explain later. You seem to be in good hands," I say sarcastically and glare at the nurse.

She finishes the wrap and smiles at him. "You're all done. Make sure you take it easy and come back if you need anything," she touches his arm again.

"Thanks," he mutters and pulls on a shirt. *Thank God … I thought she was about to drool.*

"I'm sure he'll be fine," I assure her with a flat tone. After Mak pushes his feet in his boots, he stands up weakly.

"Easy, Wren," he grins. It takes everything I have in me not to rebreak one of his ribs. I glare up at him. "Thanks again," he says to the nurse, who smiles brightly. Her bright blue eyes twinkle a little.

"Come on," I growl and lead him to the elevator. We are the only two on it.

"Was that jealousy back there?" he smirks at me.

"What would give you that impression?" I hiss.

"I've been there," he shrugs.

"It wasn't anything," I lie as the doors open.

We go to the car and I have to help him sit in the back. After I go around the other side and get in beside him, I tell the driver where to go. We get to the building and I have to help him out of the car and support him a lot of the way to apartment. When we get inside, he hobbles over to the couch and sits down slowly before flopping back and wincing. I watch him as I put my keys on the little table beside the door and go around, turning on lights.

"Nice place," he says.

"Yeah … it's lonely," I reply and sit across from him. He keeps looking around. "So, you can sleep in the bedroom. I'll take the couch. Are you hungry? You're probably hungry," I stand up.

"Wren," he huffs. I look at him. "You're rambling and being ridiculous. I'm not sleeping in your bed. I can sleep on the couch," he sighs.

"That's funny," I mumble, even though nothing was funny. "You know, I slept in your bed when I was injured so … this is my way of repaying you. Don't argue. I'm not in the mood," I growl and go to the kitchen. I open the refrigerator and look at what little is in there. Then I start to think about how the only thing I know how to make is that awful food we ate during the battle. I'm not exactly … domestic. I'm not good at anything like that. All I do is kill people and get people killed anymore …

"Everything okay?" he asks as he hobbles over to me.

"Uh … Just had a long day … lot of things on my mind. Normal stuff like war and the possibility of being attacked at any moment," I exhale.

"You're rambling again."

"Maybe we should have just left here when we had the chance. Between me and Jamison and my brothers … we could have gotten you out and just left," I continue.

"I think you need to take a deep breath," he suggests.

I look over at him.

"Take a deep breath? Are you kidding? We are completely screwed if we don't figure something out fast. How can you just tell me to take a deep breath?" I shake my head and don't even try to stop the tears from falling down my face.

"Wren, what has gotten into you?" he questions.

"Nothing ... I'm fine. It's fine." I smile and swipe the tears from my face. "I just need a minute," I brush past him and go to the bathroom. I lock the door and turn on the sink.

I sit down with my back against the door and start to cry harder. I don't know why, really. I'm driving myself crazy. One minute I'm the leader of the rising. The next, I'm a blubbering baby on the bathroom floor.

CHAPTER 15

After a while, I go to check on Wren. She's seemed off since she got me from the hospital. I don't know exactly how long I was in the prison. Days started to blur together. God knows what Wren was going through in that time. She hasn't told me anything yet. I guess I haven't really asked …

I knock on the door. I hear the water running and sniffling from the floor. I rest my forehead on the door and knock lightly. There is shuffling on the other side and the water turns off.

"Wren?"

"I'll be out soon," she replies. Her voice is thick with tears.

"Let me in," I command.

"I said I'll be out soon," she snaps.

"Come on … please just open the door," I plead. I hear more sniffling and shuffling. The door unlocks and opens a crack. "Are you going to let me in?" I ask.

"I just need a minute," she answers.

"You've had almost thirty," I scoff.

"Everything has happened too fast," she whimpers.

"You know … I was trained in psych analysis. If you open the door, I can give it a go," I chuckle.

She opens the door all the way and looks at me with the most unamused expression. Her eyes are bloodshot and puffy. Her nose is red. She looks like a total wreck. *Don't tell her that if you want to live.*

"To start, you're not looking your best," I shrug. I'm expecting a threat, but she laughs instead.

"Yeah, thanks for that," she walks past me and lays down on the couch.

"Well I'm just saying." I mutter and sit at her feet. "I've seen you look better."

She glares at me.

"Get on with it."

"You're a try-hard, Wren. And it's tearing you apart. Us humans are fragile creatures. We have to take sometimes. We can't always give," I tell her. "And sleep is crucial. By the looks of it, you haven't been doing much of that," I add.

"The only reason I've done all this was to get you back. I had to get you out of there," she shakes her head and brings her knees up to her chest. "I know how awful it is to be a prisoner there."

"And I can't thank you enough, but it's time to stop now and think about yourself," I reach over and touch her shoulder hesitantly. I'm not the best at comfort. I'm not exactly experienced in it. She says nothing for a while. I've never seen her eyes look so distant. It's like she's not even really in there and it freaks me out. She's always been so alive. Even when she was pissed as hell at me … she was *there.*

"I didn't want any of this," she murmurs. "What are we even going to do now? You're a wreck. I'm a mess. But war is coming."

"We can worry about that another time. I think right now … we need dinner," I smile. She lays back and covers her face with her hands. "Come on … let's go to your moms," I nudge her. She stands up suddenly and helps me up. We go over to her mom's apartment which is right down the hall. Her mom doesn't question Wren's puffy eyes and red nose at all. She probably knows better by now.

When we get back to her apartment, she goes to her room and changes into the pajamas that I assume were provided for her. Same with her clothes. They aren't anything she would normally wear. Everything here isn't her style. Everything is too shiny and glamorous. When she comes back out to the living room, she lays out a pillow and blanket on the couch. Wren isn't who I ever expected her to be. So much time knowing her was spent thinking she was the villain in my life and someone I had to get rid of. Now, thinking of not having her at least around … that makes me sick to my stomach. She deserves to know. She deserves some clarity.

"Can we … talk?" I clear my throat and shift uncomfortably. She looks at me for a long time before nodding and sitting on the couch. I hobble over and sit in the chair across from her. I take a deep breath and gather my thoughts. "I have more to tell you. You need to hear it."

"Yeah … okay," she croaks.

"When I was being tortured, they assumed using you was the best way to get to me. It was their go-to when they ran out of other methods. In a weakened mental state, they convinced me you were dead … and I wasn't prepared for how much that hurt. In that moment I only felt devastation. Not just because it would mean that this was all for nothing, but because it actually *hurt*. In a way, it hurt more than the whippings and the beatings. Looking back, I realize that it was so affective because … I care. I don't know why I do or –"

"Mak…" she cuts me off. I grit my teeth as she shakes her head and looks down. I know she doesn't want to hear this right now, but I press on.

"What I'm saying … is that you stopped being just a mission to me even before I turned against the New World Order. I didn't turn against them because Jamison took me and forced me to get you back, safely. He didn't even force me. It was then I started acting on my own, without thinking of the orders given to me. You weren't a mission given to me anymore. I made it my mission to keep you safe."

I watch her carefully as she stands up and comes over to me. She stands in front of me, but even sitting, I'm barely looking up at her. She hugs me awkwardly. I feel a warm tear on my neck so I hug her back as best I can. When she steps back, her eyes are bloodshot all over again. I frown up at her and think of what to say. *Well, this isn't going how I wanted.*

"We should go to sleep," she sniffles and backs away from me.

"Wait, but –"

"Mak," she cries. "Tomorrow, okay?" she smiles through the tears. I nod and stand up.

I follow her to the bedroom where she lays out a sweatpants and a tee shirt on the bed. I glance over at her. "I can sleep on the –"

"Good night," she turns on her heel and leaves without another word.

CHAPTER 16

The month that followed after bringing Maksim home from the hospital were filled with restless nights on the couch. His ribs have healed nicely, and he's started going for jogs around the outskirts of the city. President Amendola has left me to take care of him and have some time as a normal person. Maksim is exactly who I knew he could be, but it's difficult to watch him when he doesn't know I'm watching. You can take the man away from the torture, but you can't take the torture away from the man, or something like that. His eyes go somewhere else … somewhere far away. Somewhere dark.

I see the way he tenses at loud noises. I feel it when I touch his arm to help him around or when my mother puts her hand on his shoulder. I see the distrust in his eyes when my brothers are around. At night, I hear when he has a nightmare. I hear him sit up, gasping. I hear him go to the bathroom and put cold water on his face. We haven't talked further … about what he said. I haven't been able to bring myself to bring it up. He needs to get better. We both do.

"Hey … get up," Maksim nudges me. My body is stiff from the couch.

"Why?" I groan, opening my eyes. The sun has barely risen.

"I want you to come with me," he says and sits on the couch. I look up at him irritably. "You've been stuck in this apartment. Come with me," he nods towards the door. "I'm not even going fast right now. You'll be able to keep up."

I sit straight up and push the blanket off of myself. He smirks at me, knowing he got his way. He's already in his sweatpants, hoodie and sneakers. I stomp past him to my room and get dressed in running clothes and pull my hair up into a bun and go back to the living room. He's twisting his torso lightly, wincing the whole time. He's not completely healed yet.

"Ready when you are," I cross my arms.

He scoffs and goes to the door.

"Try to keep up."

The jog is mostly quiet. He'll occasionally ask questions about the rescue and "what happens now" and it really sucks that I can't completely answer everything. It is nice to get out and actually see the city. All of that peace and bliss comes to an end when the city sirens start going off.

"You've gotta be kidding me," Maksim groans. We are on the other side of the city from the apartment. "We have to leave," he grabs my wrist and starts to pull me away from the city.

"Mak, no!" I jerk away and look back at the city. You can hear the panic coming from the streets. "We can't leave," I exhale. A knot twists in my stomach and a lump forms in my throat.

"Haven't we fought with them enough?" he demands, grabbing my shoulders and shaking me a little. His eyes are frantic. He's afraid. He has every right to be afraid. "We have had our fair share of rebelling and fighting. It's time we walk away."

"My family is in there. Whatever is coming … we can handle it. We can't give them what they want," I shake my head and look back at him. He lets go of me and tugs at his hair with frustration.

"Wren, please," he begs quietly. "This is the same thing over and over again. This … it's never ending. When are we going to learn?" he growls.

"When we finish this. I can't walk away from it. It's too late!"

"I can't go back there," he trembles. My heart breaks a little. I reach for him, but he backs away. I can't ask him to fight after what they did to him. They did worse things to him than I could ever imagine. He's not even recovered yet.

"You go," I tell him. "I'll find you when it's finished. Go somewhere safe."

"You must be an idiot if you think I am going to leave you here to fight," he snaps.

"You're in no condition physically or mentally. I can't go with you. I have a responsibility for the people of this city now, whether I like it or not," I sigh. He frowns at me. "I'm sorry, Mak. Be safe," I smile sadly at him and start running for the city. He yells after me. I don't look back. It hurts to leave him, but I can't run away. I'm in too deep. Everyone in this city will be looking to me.

I don't know what it is about that little freckled face pain in the ass. She's obviously been hit in the head too many times. Somehow, she is always going to be the smartest and the dumbest person in the room at the same time. How many times is it going to take for her to learn that we can't fight these people? We always get the short end of the stick. One of us ends up being taken as a prisoner and tortured and the other has to go on some suicide mission to save the other. It's ridiculous. I don't know what's worse. The thought of going back to that hell hole myself or having her ripped away from me again, knowing everything they did to me, they will do to her times ten.

I pace back and forth, breathing slowly but I feel my heart racing. The sirens are still ringing. God only knows where Wren is now. President Amendola is probably dressing her up like a doll and putting her in front to talk our way out of this. Total bullshit. Might as well put a target on Wren's forehead.

Why aren't you going after her? They really did a number on you, to make you this scared.

My pacing stops, and I stand like a statue, staring at the city. My mouth goes dry and my skin starts to tingle. It's a familiar feeling. Back when I was a N.W.O Soldier, I would get this feeling before I had to carry on with an order I didn't exactly like. I need to stay. I hate it, but I do. If I go now, I will lose her. She'll never find her way out of this alone.

"Why did you set off the sirens if they weren't actually here yet?" I growl as President Amendola works on putting pale powder on my face and sparkly powder on my eyelids while her assistant brushes black gunk on my eyelashes.

"Because we know that they are on their way, and I want our people to get to the safe zones before they get too close. I want us to be ready," she explains.

"And why am I here?" I hiss.

"They need to see that you still stand with me and if you stand with me, it means the rest of the rebels stand with me and *that* is one big middle finger to the New World Order," she smiles softly at me and hands me a black blazer to put on over the gray dress she made me put on.

When we walk out of her office building, the streets are mostly empty. People have made their way to the safe zones. But us? We are going to stand on a stage in the middle of the city. I hug myself and scan the perimeter.

"So, how long do we wait around here?" I grumble.

"Until they show up," she growls.

We wait for a while and then see a single N.W.O Hummer driving up the main street, towards the stage. I watch President Amendola like it's my job. What does she expect to do? Just stand there and talk her way out of an attack? The driver stops right in front of the stage and gets out, holding an envelope.

"Stop," Amendola commands. The man puts his hands up defensively and looks up at her.

"I'm just delivering this from President Zurek. You must be President Amendola," he says and holds the envelope up to her.

She takes it.

"You are free to go," she grumbles and backs away from the edge of the stage. He nods and leaves without another word. She looks back at two of her guards. "Send out a patrol. I want to know if there are more waiting to attack. Report to my office when you are done," she says and turns, taking my arm and pulling me along.

"What's going on? What is that?" I question.

"We are about to find out," she grins like this excites her.

In her office, we all sit around and watch her open the envelope and read the papers that wait inside. The whole Council is in the office, cramped together along the walls. I am smushed between two other women with enough hairspray to light this whole place on fire if a single match is lit. After my patience is worn thin enough, I speak up.

"Are you going to tell us what it is?" I snap. Councilmembers give me disapproving looks.

"It's an official request for a meeting to negotiate peace," she mutters, causing the Council to celebrate. I hear relief and praises, making me sick.

"Are you all nuts? This is a trap," I step forward and grab the papers from Amendola. I read over them, shaking my head the whole time. "It's a trap. They are just trying to catch us off guard," I growl as her security comes in. Amendola looks at them, ignoring me for the moment.

"Nothing, Ma'am. There is nothing. We will keep patrols out through the night," one says. Amendola thanks and dismisses them before turning her attention back to me.

"We have to take the chance," she shrugs and takes the papers back from me.

"You're kidding," *Silence.* "If you are honestly considering this, you're not as intelligent as I thought," I spit and begin to pace in the small space available.

"Maybe I'm not … but this is a chance at peace and I'm willing to risk it," she sighs and sits in her chair. I open my mouth to argue but give it up and storm out.

After finding my way to my apartment through the angry tears in my eyes, I practically have a heart attack when Maksim grabs me as soon as I walk in the door.

"Maksim, what are you doing?" I demand, grabbing his arms to hold myself up.

"I didn't know where you were, so I came back here," he tells me and searches my face. I brush past him and go to the bedroom, stumbling out of the heels. "Wren, what happened?" he asks, following. I pull out pajamas and toss them on the bed, running my hands through my hair.

"She's so stupid," I grumble, storming into the bathroom and turning on the sink.

I rip off my blazer and stick my hands under the water and splash it on my face to wash off the makeup I was painted in. I look at my reflection. I'm suddenly a racoon. Maksim is watching with a worried expression and his arms crossed over his body. He's still in his running clothes. He hasn't done anything since I ran off, except come back here. If he were smart, he would have left. I wipe my face with a towel, but the mascara is still around my eyes. I ignore it and go back to the bedroom. Before Maksim can come back in, I close and lock the door.

"Wren, talk to me. I can't help if you just ramble on," he says irritably.

I change into the pajamas, throwing my dress to the side. I rip open the door and storm into the living room, flopping on the couch with a huff.

"Amendola doesn't use her head and she's going to get us all killed," I groan. He sits beside me calmly, saying nothing. "Zurek had someone deliver a formal request for a meeting to negotiate peace. On New World Order Territory," I throw my hands up and tug at my hair.

"I need you to take about ten steps back and explain this to me," he sighs and touches my shoulder. I shrug him off and cross my arms.

"Zurek sent a letter to Amendola with a personal delivery boy. It's a letter to her requesting a meeting between the two Council's to negotiate a peace treaty," I grumble.

"So? No leader in their right mind would take that offer. Not from Zurek," he scoffs. I look over at him and wait for him to connect the dots. His smirk fades. "You're kidding me," his face falls.

"She's accepting it," I tell him.

"Listen to me, Wren," he snaps, sitting up and grabbing my shoulders. "If she asks you to come, you say no. Do you understand? You say no! You can't go! They *will* kill you!" he shakes me a little.

"I may not be given a choice, Mak!" I yell and shove his hands off of me.

"Can we leave now?" he demands.

"Just get up and go? Go where? What about my family, Maksim?" I stand up.

"Once they get out of the safe zones, we find them and go!"

"Not until I get my orders from President Amendola," I shake my head and look down.

He stands up and stomps to the bedroom door. "Like it or not, Wren, you've become her little pet. And that's not the you I –" he stops and looks away. I hug myself and shift my weight from foot to foot. "That's not the you I risked everything for," he finishes and goes into the bedroom, slamming the door.

I sink down on the couch and pull my knees up to my chin and pull my blanket over myself. I squeeze my eyes shut and clutch the blanket until sleep finally eases me away from all of this.

CHAPTER 17

I give up on sleep shortly before dawn. I get up and go to the living room where Wren is curled up in the corner of the couch. Her eyes are puffed up and her face is flushed. I sit beside her and listen to her breathing. It's soft and slow. For once, she isn't fidgeting or biting the inside of her cheek nervously. My eyes fall shut and my breathing comes to match hers.

I don't know how much time passes, but when I feel her start to stir and open my eyes, the sun is much higher in the sky. Wren turns, leaning her back against me and her head falls onto my chest. I stop breathing for a second. She's still fast asleep, but she may not like me being here right now. I watch her for a little longer and then decide to get up. I slowly try to slide away, and she wakes up, inhaling deeply and stretching her arms out. I swear under my breath as she opens her eyes.

"Hi," she says groggily.

"I was just about to get up," I blurt out.

She draws her brows together and sits up.

"Okay, then," she mumbles and pushes the blanket off herself.

"Did you sleep okay?" I ask as I get up, so I don't have to look her in the eye.

"Yeah … I guess. I see you didn't," she follows me into the kitchen. "You look like shit," she adds. I turn and see a slight smile on her face. I roll my eyes. "Why were you –"

"Let's not talk about it," I cut her off.

Her smile drops and she nods, turning away.

"Let me know if Amendola calls," she sighs and goes into the bathroom. I hear the shower turn on and lean back against the counter.

She's stuck under Isabelle's thumb and it's ruining her chance at finally being free. It's ruining her mom and brother's chance at being free. If she told them she wanted to leave, they wouldn't think twice. They would drop everything for her. *I* would drop everything.

I go down the hall to Elissa's apartment. She welcomes me in, but I can see the worry in her eyes. We sit down at her dining table and she folds her hands, ready to listen.

"I'm worried about Wren. She's becoming a puppet. President Amendola's puppet. We need to get her out of here before she gets killed for that woman," I tell her.

She looks down and nods.

"For once you and Heath agree then," she sighs and smiles sadly. "There's nothing we can do, Maksim. Wren does the opposite of what anyone tells her. She can't be controlled," she says through tears. "I know why you're scared. I know why you want to get her out of here. I do too. But I can't. Heath and Alec can't. Mak … even you can't. We can't push her. It'll just push her away," she shrugs and wipes tears from the corners of her eyes.

I look down and nod.

"So, what do we do?" I ask.

"We stand behind her … and fight with her."

"This … it's not good. She's going to get hurt," I shake my head.

"There's no stopping her," she sighs. "She is going to do what she thinks it right. And that's going to be what Amendola tells her is right."

"So, that's it then? We let her go?" I demand. She doesn't respond, so I take that as a yes. "When we lose her … *again* … it is going to be harder to get her back alive," I snap.

"I'm sorry I missed your call," I tell her and adjust my shirt.

She smiles and waves her hand.

"Water under the bridge, Wren. You're here now. And you dressed properly on your own. Well done," she praises me like a child.

"Why did you ask me here?" I cross my arms.

"We are going to negotiate peace again … and I need you to come with me," she says.

I feel my heart begin to race.

"Zurek will kill me on sight," I snap.

"No one will be harmed," she shakes her head calmly.

"Isabelle, I ruined everything for him! I turned everything upside down! It's all my fault!" I cry.

"I understand why you're scared, Wren –"

"No! You don't! You don't know what it's like to be chained in a cell and tortured every day! You don't know what it's like to have your mind altered! They led Maksim to believe I was dead! They broke him! *Him,*" I am practically screaming. She doesn't understand. She could never understand.

"They broke you too, Wren. You can say it," she says calmly. Here she goes again. Making me the damaged little girl in need of protection. I would like to see her with a gun.

"But that doesn't mean anything. I stopped doing this for myself a long time ago. I'm doing this for what they did to the people I love. They hurt my mom. They killed my brother, Mason. They put Maksim through the deepest depths of Hell," I hiss, swiping tears from my face.

"So, come with me. Look them in the eye and show them that they didn't win. This isn't surrender, Wren. This is a victory for us. We get peace, finally," she beams.

"I don't want peace anymore. I want revenge," I growl and look away from her.

"It's a slippery slope. Go home … rest on it. Let me know by tomorrow. We leave the day after," she sighs and turns away from me in her chair.

I dismiss myself and storm home. I pass people and receive several worried glances as I pass by. These people don't know real pain and fear. No one here gets it. Heath and Alec hardly get it. Mom gets it. Mak gets it.

Upon entering the apartment, I immediately wish I could turn and run back out, but between Heath and Maksim, I wouldn't stand a chance.

"Have a seat, honey," mom smiles and pats the seat beside her on the couch. I hesitantly join her. Mak sits on the other side of me. I feel trapped. My brother's sit across from us. Alec can't meet my eyes and Heath is just glaring at Mak, but what else is new.

"Is this some sort of intervention?" I scoff.

"Not this time," Heath snorts.

"What's going on? Maksim?" I look over at Mak, who also isn't meeting my eyes. We had an argument about him not answering Amendola while I was in the shower earlier. I didn't think he would still be hung up on it.

"Did Amendola ask you to go with her?" he asks, raising his eyes to meet mine. I nod and swallow the lump in my throat. "What did you say?"

"I'm giving her my answer tomorrow," I look over to my brother's. Heath looks at Maksim, but not with a glare this time. When I look at Mak, he shrugs to Heath. "What?" I snap. Mak smiles slightly to Heath, which is not returned, but Heath sits forward.

"You have a duty to Amendola now. As a Free World Protector, you have to do exactly that. Even if it means going against your own desires. You should go with her and the Council to the negotiation. She won't let anything happen to her face of the Free World," he tells me.

"It's not just about what I want. It's not safe. I didn't think any of you would be fond of me going," I shake my head.

"We will make sure whatever guards she takes keep an eye on you especially," mom says softly.

I look to Alec, who nods in agreement and gives me a reassuring smile. Mom squeezes my hand and is going on about how much power I really have if I can put my feelings aside and do what is right for the greater good. Heath nods along, but Maksim is a statue beside me.

"What do you think?" I blurt out, looking over at him.

He doesn't look me directly in the eye for too long and he fiddles with his sleeves.

"It's completely your choice," he answers tightly.

"Mak," I pry my hand from my mothers and grab his. "You freaked out last night at the thought of me going. What's changed?" I growl. "Don't lie."

"I'm with you. I told you I would support you and that's what I'm doing," he shakes his head and clenches his jaw.

"I don't believe you. You can say no. You can tell me not to go," I choke.

"Maksim," Heath growls.

"Why? Why do you need me to support this?" Mak snaps, standing abruptly. "It's not like you've cared before when you've made stupid decisions!"

I look around at the others and shrug.

"We've been through a lot and it would help to know you trust me … but clearly you don't," I mutter and stand up to leave.

He catches my arm.

"How is this about trust?" he demands.

"You don't trust me to do what needs to be done!" I shout, resisting the urge to start a real fight.

"It's Amendola and Zurek I don't trust, Wren. You can't be that stupid," he spits. I try to jerk away, but his grip is too tight.

"Get your hands off of her," Heath commands, standing up.

"Back off!" I yell at Heath and shove Mak in the chest with my free arm. He lets go and I am out of that apartment faster than a bat out of Hell. I hear the yelling from the apartment as I bolt down the hall and down the stairs.

I don't know how long I walk around the city before deciding it's time to go back. It's dark and getting colder the longer the sun isn't out. I hug myself and sulk back into the apartment building. I notice two of Amendola's guards in the lobby. They nod to each other when they see me and go back to pretending to read magazines. I take the stairs up to the apartment. The door is open when I get there.

My mom and Amendola are sitting at the dining table and my brothers are slouched on the couch. They all look at me and stand when I take a step inside. Mak comes out from the bedroom. I notice a new bruise on his jawline and take a second look at Heath. His eye is black and blue along with his right knuckles. *Of course, they got into a fist fight.*

"What are you doing here?" I ask Isabelle.

"Your family wanted to be sure that you would be safe during the negotiation," she smiles.

"I asked her to come," mom sighs.

"What time do we leave?" I mutter and close the apartment door.

"Mid-morning the day after tomorrow. Dress professionally, but still comfortable," she nods and comes closer to me, touching my shoulder. "This is really a good thing you are doing, Wren."

"I'll see you then," I brush past her to the kitchen and get a glass of water. After she leaves, my blood begins to boil with anger again. I feel all eyes on me and it irks me. "Go home. The three of you, get out. Go home. Maksim and I need to talk," I growl.

Heath whispers something to Maksim. Probably a threat. Alec gives me a sympathetic smile as he leaves, followed by mom and then Heath. Once they are gone, Maksim locks the door for the night. He turns to me hesitantly.

"I'm –"

"Who threw the first punch?" I cut him off.

"Who threw the first punch, or who landed the first punch?" he smirks.

"Don't be smart with me right now, I swear, or I will start throwing punches and I won't miss." I say in a warning tone.

He flops back on the couch and sighs.

"He did," he answers, rolling his eyes.

"Does it hurt?"

"Not as much as it should," he mutters, tugging on his hair, hiding his face. I grab an icepack from the freezer and sit beside him.

"Here," I hold it over to him. He mutters a thanks and presses it against his jaw. "You don't get it do you?" I sigh. He looks over at me, saying nothing. "You're the only one with the guts to tell me when something is a bad idea, Mak. I rely on you for that. You overthink enough for the both of us and I need you to overthink for me, because I don't think enough. I jump into things without thinking. I jumped into being with Jeremy and then I jumped into trying to kill him. I jumped into this rebellion … I jumped into *you*," I whimper.

He looks down at me.

"But somehow all of it worked out to some extent. You don't need me, Wren," he tells me.

"One day it won't work out. And I do. I promise you … I do," I insist and rest my elbows on my knees. There is a gaping hole in the middle of my chest, and it aches.

"I think this negotiation is an awful idea. I think it's a trap. But I know why it's important for you to be there," he says, putting the ice pack down. "Even if it means putting you in danger."

"So, what do I do?" I groan and lean back, frustrated.

"You go. And you look that bastard in the eye and show him you aren't scared and then you do what's right and you help bring peace.

That's what this rebellion was all about from the start," he nudges me and tries a reassuring smile.

I nod.

"What are you going to do?" I ask.

"Sit and wait for you to get back as patiently as possible," he shrugs.

"And if I don't come back?" I chuckle dryly, though nothing is funny.

"Kiss peace goodbye and start a real war," he responds with a distant look in his eye.

"I'm sorry Heath punched you," I say after a long silence. He shrugs as if to say it's no big deal. *He's been through worse.*

"I would love nothing more ... than to see the New World Order symbol burning in flames with everyone who ever had anything to do with it," He mumbles out of nowhere.

"You had something to do with it," I counter.

"And I stand by what I said," he sighs.

I roll my eyes.

"You're being dramatic. I mean I get it, but you got out. You left. You chose a better path –"

"That doesn't change anything I have done, Wren!" he yells. "*You* don't get it," he adds.

"What?" I croak.

He looks over at me with an expression of self-disgust.

"When was the last time you looked someone in the eye right before taking their life? When was the last time you pried a child from their mother's arms while the child cried, begging her to help them?" he questions and then laughs like a mad man. "When was the last time you tortured someone just because you could?" his eyes search my face frantically. "Have you ever watched someone's soul leave their eyes by your hand?" he growls and looks away, shaking his head. He looks like he is going to be sick to his stomach. "Someone like you could never understand how I feel. I disgust myself," he shrugs, defeated.

"You –"

"Don't try to justify what I've done, Wren, it's insulting," he puts his hand up to stop me. "Besides, I saw the disgust in your eyes when you found out who I really was," he smiles sadly down at the floor. "How could I forget that?"

"Are you done?" I ask. He glances at me. "It's never too late to right the wrongs you have done. You're moving in the right direction and I think you need to give yourself some more credit for that. And for the record, I was never disgusted with you. I was just hurt. But you've been forgiven. By me ... by Jamison and my mom. By all the rebels. You've found where you belong. I hope it starts to be enough for you," I whisper because my voice won't allow anything more.

"You should get some sleep," he grumbles, walking away.

Suppressing the urge to scream in frustration, I give up and get ready for bed. I lay out the pillow and blanket on the couch and go to the bathroom to change. When I come back out, Maksim is laying on the couch.

"Maksim –"

"Night," he interrupts and turns over on his side. I turn out the light and go into the bedroom.

CHAPTER 18

"Hey there, Rebel," a vaguely familiar voice says as I get into one of the SUV's.

"Brookes? Why are you coming?" I hiss, annoyed with his presence.

"President Amendola wants someone there to cover this moment, firsthand," he beams. I grumble under my breath and look out the window. "Have I done something to upset you?" he asks after the SUV train leaves the city.

"What you do … I don't like it," I tell him. "You make the Free World seem so great and perfect to everyone on the outside. But really it has its own problems and corruption," I explain.

"Corruption?" he laughs.

"I know secrecy when I see it," I glare over at him.

He smiles and nods.

"Well, I'm sorry you feel that way. I'm just doing my job," he looks out his window.

"Yeah … me too," I murmur and watch the desolation pass as we drive towards the New World Order. My stomach twists the closer we get. When I see the concrete slab tower past rubble, I know we have arrived.

Why did President Amendola agree to do this *here* in their territory? I'm sure Zurek sweet talked her into coming here.

We get to the main Council building and Isabelle's best security team surrounds us. Most of the Free World Council came along with Ivan Brookes and me. We walk in to the building and see what is left of the New World Order Council. President Zurek is in the middle of them all with a smug smile on his face.

"Welcome," he says and stands. Amendola goes up to him and shakes his hand. She turns to me and motions me to join her at the table. Our Council takes their seats, leaving on open beside Isabelle for me. I hesitantly sit down, not taking my eyes off of Zurek. "Nice to see you again, Miss Adler," he holds his hand over to me.

"Unfortunately, I can't say the same," I growl, ignoring his handshake. Amendola glares over at me with disapproval.

"Well, then. We should get down to business," he shuffles through papers.

Our guards stand behind us, staring down N.W.O Soldiers behind their Council. Amendola and Zurek do most of the talking. Other Councilmembers on both sides will speak on certain topics briefly, but I sit and watch everyone around me. I have nothing to say. Nothing helpful at least.

"And now your last condition," Amendola sighs.

Zurek nods to two of his Soldiers, who start to move around to our side of the table. I sit up on edge and look around. None of the Free World Councilmembers can't look me in the eye. Ivan looks just as confused as me. Before I know it, the Soldiers grab me and pull me out of the chair.

"What the hell?!" I snap, thrashing around.

"You're making the right decision, President Amendola," Zurek smiles and stands up, buttoning his suit jacket. Amendola stands up too and shakes his hand.

"Isabelle!" I scream.

She turns to me.

"I'm sorry Wren. I told you ... my people come before one person, always. I had to do this. I hope you can understand," she frowns.

Ivan gapes as I am dragged away, kicking and screaming. This was the plan the whole time. She turned me in so there wouldn't be war. I was willing to negotiate peace, but not like this. What is my family going to think? Does she think Mak and Heath won't wonder where I am? I can't sit around and wait for them to come rescue me. I need to get myself out of this one.

"What do you mean she ran off? Why would Wren run off?" Heath demands.

President Amendola lowers her eyes.

"I wish I knew," she sighs. "I just wanted to let you all know. I hope she comes back soon," she adds and turns away from the door.

Heath and I watch her walk down the hallway and then close the door. We look back at Elissa, who is in shock. Alec paces behind her anxiously. Heath and I look at each other for a long time. It's like we are reading each other's minds. Our jaws clench simultaneously, and we nod.

"Something happened," I growl.

Elissa looks between us frantically. Her eyes begin to water.

"What? President Amendola said she just ran off. Maybe … maybe she just got upset and is on her way back here. Wren … she's impulsive," she rambles.

"Mom," Heath sighs and touches her shoulder. He shakes his head and sits down beside her. "She wouldn't do that … knowing we were so worried about this negotiation. Something had to of happened," he says gently.

"What do you think could have happened?" Alec snaps. "What would President Amendola have let happen to her?"

"She said she would do anything for her people," I shrug.

Heath looks at me and nods.

"Zurek would love to punish Wren for what she started. All he needed was for her to be handed over," he says.

"What do we do?" Alec mutters. "We can't just take Amendola's word for it can we? We have to go find her, wherever she is," he says.

Heath nods.

"What if she is in the prison?" he asks.

"She managed to get half of the rebels out of there with an entire team. The three of us can get her out," I shrug. We all look at each other for a long time.

"We need to tell Jamison." Elissa cries. We all agree and go back to looking at each other.

I can't express what I'm feeling exactly. Part of me wants to vomit … the other part wants to run my fist through a wall. I've never been so tired in my life. This time is going to be different. This time, when we get her back, we are all going somewhere, far away from the New World Order and the Free World. No more Presidents. No more Councils. No more uniforms or fancy clothes to hide the lies.

And this time, I'm burning the New World Order down and the Free World Order can burn with them in Hell.

After getting Jamison sobered up and in working condition, we tell him our theory. He mumbles gibberish about the New World Order taking everything from him. I want to knock sense into the old man. He's been going downhill slowly.

"Jamison!" I yell, making him glare up at me. "Back in the abandoned city when we faced the New World Order Army ... Jackson knew you and you knew him. How?" I demand.

"You haven't figured it out yet, Soldier?" he grins like a madman. "I was in his unit for years. When I came to my senses and realized how wrong it all was ... I left. Jackson was my friend. I tried to bring him with me. We were younger then, and he was even colder than he is now ... but he let me go without reporting me. I left him behind and turned against him," he tells me. *Once a soldier, always a soldier.* "I know just as well as anybody how awful the New World Order is."

"That's why you've forgiven me," I mutter. He smiles with more sanity and gentleness. "Can you stay sober long enough to get Wren back? It's not too late for her, Jamison. Mary would want you to come with us," I say firmly.

He gets a distant look in his eye and is quiet for a long time. "Let's give em' hell."

"Let me out of here!" I scream and flail against the restraints. Other prisoners groan as they wait to be executed. At this point I rather be executed then kept here to be tortured. "What do you want with me?" I demand. Boots stomp down the hallway and stop outside my cell.

"Shut up, Wren," a Soldier taps on the bars with his gun. His voice is familiar. I look closely in the dark.

Jeremy.

"You bastard ..." I gape at him. "Why are you here? Why are you helping them?!" I demand.

"You're not the brightest all the time, Wren. I was never really with you and your little Reformation. I was getting information because Maksim failed. When I knew the bombers were coming, I got out of there and came back here. I told them everything I knew and earned my rightful spot here with the New World Order," he tells me.

"Maksim is going to kill you when he gets here," I shake my head in utter disbelief.

"He's not coming. He thinks you ran off. He thinks you chose not to go back to him," he smiles and leans against the bars.

"Jeremy, let me go. I will go. I will get my family and we will vanish. You'll never have to see us again. I promise," I plead.

"Oh Wren. This isn't about not having to deal with you. This is about revenge," he sighs.

"I can't believe this. I can't believe you. How long have you been planning this?" I hiss.

"Since you decided to go completely crazy," he shrugs. I look at the ceiling and try to slow my breathing. "You did this. You did all of this. Everything they did to Maksim and you and everyone you care about ... it's all because of you," he says coldly.

"So, what? You're just going to kill me?" I scoff.

"As well as Maksim, your brothers and your mother," he nods.

"Please ... you don't have to do that. If you kill me, it'll all be over. There is no reason to kill them," I ramble.

"We both know that isn't the case. Maksim will come seeking revenge for killing you. And with him, your brothers. And your mom, as precious of a woman as she is, she's a loose end that will need to be cut," he explains. As if I didn't know what would really happen if they killed me. *When they kill you.*

"Please ... don't. I'm begging you. Just leave them," I plead.

"You know I can't, and let's be real, Wren. You know I want Maksim gone. You and him ... you became a big problem together. He's had it coming."

"How dramatic do you have to be, Jeremy. Threatened by another male because he got close to what you *thought* was yours? I'm not anyone's anything. If that's what this is about –"

"It's not!" he snaps. "This is for the good of the New World Order!

This is to show anyone who dare defy against us what *will* happen! No one beats us!" he explodes.

"When? When do you kill me? And how?" I demand.

"Tomorrow. High noon. Publicly hanged," he answers. I let my head fall back against the cold wall in defeat. "You put up a good fight, Wren. But I always told you this would happen. I told you your ambitions would get you killed. You should have just kept your head down and doodled your way through life," he adds before leaving me alone.

Hours later, I hear doors open and the shuffling of feet. A woman's voice asks what is going on. The guard tells her that there is someone she should meet before they are hanged.

"Enjoy your last night of company," the guard spits at me as he shoves the woman into the cell. *Why doesn't she have to be chained up?* She looks like she's been a prisoner for a long time. She's nothing but skin and bone. Her eyes are sunken in and her hair is matted and a tangled mess. Something about her is familiar.

"Who are you?" she asks me. Her voice is shallow and hoarse.

"Wren Adler."

"*You're* Wren Adler?" she gasps and sits in front of me. I nod, unsure if it's a good time to be me or not. "You know my son," she insists.

"Who's your son?" I mutter.

"Maksim. Maksim Ozera," she beams.

It feels like someone just punched me in the gut. Her eyes ... they are just like his eyes. That's what was familiar ... but she's supposed to be dead. I gape at her in silence for a long time.

"Maksim told me you died ... from the sickness," I shake my head in disbelief.

"That's what everyone thinks. Everyone except my husband's inner circle and a few of these guards," she tells me.

"I've been here before ... I've never seen you."

"He's kept me in solitary confinement," she frowns. "I don't know why they wanted me to meet you," she mumbles.

"Because I'm going to be hanged tomorrow. And I'll never have the chance to tell Maksim that his mother is alive," I grumble.

"How's Sonia?" she asks after a long silence. *Oh God ...*

"You don't know?" I whimper. She tilts her head, confused. "She was killed … in a bombing," I tell her. Her face falls. "I'm so sorry, Mrs. Ozera."

"Please … call me Katherine," she forces a polite smile. "They told me you and Maksim became close," she changes the subject.

"We got close … yeah," I smile and nod.

"There was talk of his mission. To use you to get to the rebellion. The son I raised would have never even considered it," she tells me.

"Well … I doubt he was the same person you raised when he was assigned that mission," I smile to myself. "I just hope he's finding his way back to what he knows is right."

"If he chose the rebellion in the end … he is," she touches my knee gently. "It just took someone strong to show him the right path."

"It took more than that," I scoff. There is silence for a long time. I think back on the past year. This can't be the end. Not after everything all of us have been through. "How do I get out of this, Katherine?" I whimper. She looks down at the ground and sighs, thinking for a long time. I do my best to keep my composure, but every part of me wants to curl up in a ball and cry.

"I wish I knew, sweetheart. I never thought much about it. Once I was put down here, I knew for me, there was no escaping and surviving. I had nowhere to go," she whispers.

"So, that's it then. I'm going to die," I mutter.

"Wren," she smiles softly. "I also didn't have anyone to save me. Maksim is smart. Whatever he has been told about your disappearance … I'm sure he's caught on," she winks. *How is her spirit still so alive after years of being locked away by her own husband? And for what?*

"If I do get out of here … you're coming with me."

"If you get the opportunity to get out of here, you run, and you never look back. Don't waste time coming for me." *It wouldn't be a waste.*

CHAPTER 19

"Amendola can't know our plan to leave. She can't know that we've left at all. If this is going to work, we have to be fast and leave during shift change," I tell everyone. Heath and Alec nod in agreement. Elissa looks like she's going to be sick and I don't think Jamison is able to feel anything at the moment, still. "Midnight is when guards switch out. We should be ready to bolt out of the city walls shortly before that."

"Wait, bolt?" Heath shakes his head. I nod. "Why don't we steal a SUV? I could grab keys before evening," he shrugs.

"It's easier to see a car leaving, rather than people in the night."

"It's also easier to outrun another car if we are in one," he growls.

"Isabella Amendola isn't stupid. I'm sure she has trackers on every vehicle. We have a better chance of making it to Wren if we go by foot. At least to the train tracks," I explain.

"Why the train tracks?" Elissa asks.

"It's a day's drive to the New World Order from here in a car. If we hop the train, it'll be faster, but we have to run to it by two a.m."

"You've lost your damn mind. We can't hop a train going that fast!" Heath snaps.

"If you would all let me finish," I snap back and lay out a map. "The train tracks run through these low grounds. There is a cliff that runs along the tracks. If we can get there before the train comes through, we can wait and practically step onto it. When it stops in the N.W.O station, we go," I sigh.

"We could die, did you take that into consideration?" Alec grumbles. *The boy hardly ever speaks and when he does, this is the shit that comes out.*

"Do you know what the train carries, Alec?" *Silence.* "Grain. Cars and cars of grain. *Open* cars," I hiss.

"How were we supposed to know? We didn't used to work for the enemy," Heath barks.

"You three need to knock it off," Jamison warns. We look at him. He rubs his temples and squeezes his eyes shut. "We officially have the same goal. We are on the same page. We are on the same *team* and that means you three need to start acting like it," he lectures. I look down and bite my tongue.

"So ... we leave tonight," Elissa says. We all nod. "And what happens when we get there?"

"Soldier?" Jamison looks to me grinning.

"Thanks to Wren and Jamison, we aren't without protection. After my rescue mission, they kept a few guns for themselves in case we would need them," I open one of the kitchen cabinets and smile back at the others. "Do any of you remember how you got into the prison before?" I ask.

"We took the sewer tunnels. There was a door into the prison basement where you and the others were kept," he answers.

"Then that's how we will get in again. I don't want us firing our guns if we don't have to, especially in a tunnel. Be prepared to fight with your hands."

"What if we are too late? What if she is already gone to be executed?" Heath questions. I look at him and see the fear in his eyes. As horrible as he can be to deal with, he loves Wren. He would do anything to protect her and I respect that. I understand him.

"Then it's a good thing we have these guns. We go for her. We kill anyone that gets in our way," I assure him. He gives me a fleeting half smile. "I can't promise any of you that we will be successful," I look at the others. "But I can promise that I will do anything to get her out of there alive," Everyone looks down and nods in agreement. I take a deep breath. "With that said... if it comes down to someone staying behind ... to give her a chance at escape ... it's going to be me."

"No, Maksim," Jamison snaps.

"No questions asked," I snap back. "As soon as we get her, you run, and you get her far away from the New World Order and far away from the Free World. Don't stop until you are so far, it's impossible to be tracked. Don't stop until you are somewhere the New World Order will never dare go. And for the love of God … do not look back. No matter what," I order.

"Maksim …" Heath mumbles. I look at him. "Even if *we* agreed to that … Wren would never let us leave you behind. She wouldn't have it," he squeezes my shoulder.

"Are you telling me between the four of you, you couldn't drag her away from all of this? I don't care if you have to tie her up and keep her in a locked room. Do not let her ever come back. No matter what," I am practically begging.

"She'll hate us," Alec shakes his head.

"Let her. It's better she hate you and be *safe* … then get her way and end up dead," my throat feels raw at the thought of her dying over something stupid like coming back *again* to save me. "We are never going to get out of this cycle of rescue missions if someone doesn't draw the line. I'm drawing that line," I croak.

"Let's just hope no one has to stay behind," Jamison intervenes.

"Where do we go … once we get her back?" Alec asks me. He has the same fear in his eyes as his brother.

"South," Jamison answers. I look at him. "The coast. At least for a little while. It's out of New World Order Territory and has resources we could live off of until we make another move. The rebels that survived stayed there after the battle," he tells me.

"That should work for a little while. If we are fast enough, we can get back on the train before it departs. It goes south before turning around. It'll get us far enough before we have to walk the rest of the way. Give us some time and distance."

"Alright. Everyone should rest before we have to get out of here," Elissa blurts and walks out of the kitchen and over to the bedroom. Heath and Alec exchange glances before going to the couch. Jamison stands from the dining table and pats my shoulder.

I go to the bedroom and knock on the side of the doorframe. Elissa smiles back at me. I step in and shove my hands in my pockets.

"We'll get her back. This plan gives us time and they don't know we are coming. We have a chance," I reassure her.

She holds one of Wren's sweaters in her hands, close to her body. "I want to thank you … for all of this," she whispers.

"There's been too many rescue missions over the past year. It has to stop."

"I need to ask something of you," she sighs and glances over my shoulder. I look back at Heath and Alec. Their eyes are closed, and their heads are back. "I want to be the one to stay … if someone has to. Let it be me," she says.

"Absolutely not."

"Maksim … I am her mother. I stood against her for too long. When she was a child … I *let* her father take out his anger on her and I have never done anything to make up for all of it."

"She will never forgive me if I let you stay behind," I argue.

"Listen to me," she snaps. "If someone has to, it's going to be me. You can protect her better than I can. She needs you. Through all of this, it's been you and her –"

"And we see how that has continuously turned out!"

"She will never stop trying to fight for you. Even if they kill you, she will want revenge and she will always be in danger. If she has you and her brothers, she will learn how to live a normal life. You can give her a normal life. Please … if it comes down to it … let it be me," she pleads. *She will never let it go if her mom dies at the hands of the New World Order. But she gets her stubbornness from somewhere, and I think I see where now.*

"Fine … but only if it comes down to it," I agree, reluctantly.

"Thank you," she slouches onto the bed and hugs Wren's sweater. My stomach twists into knots. I've never been the best at sticking to my religion. I've done awful things despite it. But I pray that it doesn't come down to someone staying behind.

"The guards are leaving to clock out. Now."

We run, staying low and moving fast. We stay away from lights and keep to the outskirts of the city. Once we are outside the walls, we switch to a full sprint, heading south-east. My body aches not long after we start, but I keep pushing. A year ago, this would have been nothing. I could run for hours and feel nothing. After being a prisoner and tortured, my body has gotten weak and hasn't healed completely. I can only think of Wren and what they could be doing to her right now. I should have made her stay …

As we reach the cliff, we can hear the train coming. We climb down to the widest ledge and wait. My heart pounds and I can feel my blood rushing through my head. The train starts to fly past us and car after car passes. Jamison starts to count and on three, we all jump. Our bodies, though landing on wheat, are thrown back from the speed of the train, but we are all fine. *There is a God.*

The ride to the New World Order station takes a few hours. We get there by dawn. I'll skip the details of our exit from the train and to the tunnel entrance. Its anxiety inducing, that much I will say. There are Soldiers around every corner, and I practically hold my breath the entire time. Once we are in the tunnels, we take a minute to breathe.

"We are so close," Heath whispers. There is a ringing in my ears. Adrenaline tells me to run and not stop until we get to Wren. "The door is a few yards that way," he points and I nod.

"Lead the way," I tell him.

Heath and I take up the front. Alec protects our backs. Jamison and Elissa stay close to each other, both looking scared as hell. When we get to the door, Heath opens it slowly, but it creeks loudly, making me swear under our breath. *They may not have known we were here before, but they will now.*

CHAPTER 20

Katherine and I perk up when we hear the door that leads to the tunnel creek open. The Soldier on guard duty comes out of the office and his face looks like he's seen a ghost. Katherine stands and presses her face against the bars and gasps.

"Ozera," the soldier spits.

"Maksim ..." Katherine looks back at me, beaming. My heart is filled with joy and fear.

With him, my brothers, mom and Jamison come down the long hall with the guns that Jamison and I kept. I can't help but smile, though my stomach is twisted in knots. The soldier turns to call for backup, but Maksim reaches him before he can and in one swift motion, he snaps the guard's neck. I watch him crumble and hit the ground with a dull thud. Maksim looks in the cell and his face loses any color there was when he sees his mother. Heath grabs the keys from the guard's belt and Alec goes into the office. Jamison stands watching both entrance points with his gun up and ready to fire.

"Mom ..." Maksim exhales.

"I know this is a shock to you, Maksim, but please, focus," she orders. He looks past her at me as Heath opens the door. The two of them come in and work on unchaining me. They lower my arms from over my head and unlock the chains from my wrists and ankles.

"Guys, guards are coming," Alec calls from the office.

"Help me hide the body," Jamison growls. My mother runs into the cell and pulls me to my feet, hugging me tight. Maksim just looks at his mom, saying nothing. Heath and Jamison drag the guard's body to one of the cells and start bickering about what to do next.

"Wren," My mom pulls back, gripping my shoulders. "Switch clothes with me," she says frantically. "Don't ask questions, just do it," she starts taking off her boots and jacket. "Now, Wren!" I do as I am told not thinking. I take off the prison jump suit and pull on her jeans and jacket over my tee shirt.

"What are you doing?" I question, against her order not to.

"When they get down here, they will need to see you here, still or they will go on the hunt for you. I'm taking your place," she tells me.

"Mom, no! Heath, tell her no!" I cry. He looks between us, torn. Maksim is still in shock, looking between his mother and mine. "Someone do something. Let's just go! All of us!"

Katherine looks at my mom and they share some sort of mom telepathy. I can see it.

My mom grabs Maksim's shoulders and shakes him into focus. "Get her out of here and keep her safe," she snaps. "Do not let her come back, no matter what, do you hear me?" He nods numbly. "Promise me!" She yells. He mumbles a promise with another nod.

She turns and hugs me before Katherine puts the chains on my mother's ankles and wrists. Katherine shoves us out of the cell and hugs Maksim, whispering something to him that I don't hear. Tears are blurring my vision and my legs feel like gelatin. Katherine closes the door and sits beside my mother like she was sitting beside me.

"Maksim, please, we have to get them both out of here," I beg, gripping his arm for support.

He looks down at me with tears in his eyes. "She asked me to keep you safe," he mutters. "I promised her I would," he practically drags me down the hall to the door.

I'm too weak to kick or scream, but I cry. Heath and Alec follow like zombies and Jamison ushers us forward. We get into the tunnel and Jamison closes the door. He puts a finger up to his lips and we stand silent. Maksim keeps his hands tight around my arms and refuses to look at me as I cry and quietly beg him to go back and get both of our mother's. Soldiers voices are muffled, but I hear them say that the guard that was on duty must have left his post and we listen to them leave.

"Maksim, please, please, *please*. We can go get them now before more come back," I sob.

He searches my face, pained, but says nothing. He pulls me against him and hugs me tight to keep me from squirming away. "I'm so sorry," he mumbles into my hair.

"They'll figure it out if we do that Wren," Jamison says, pushing us towards the exit from the tunnel. "We have to go *now.*"

Maksim continues to drag me along, having to keep me on my feet and begging me to stop crying. As we reach the ladder, I crumble. He sinks to the ground, holding me like a child.

"She shouldn't have to pay for what I've done."

"Wren, please… we have to get out of here. I *need* to get you away from this place," he insists, holding my face in his hands. I suck in deep breaths as hot tears soak my cheeks and his hands.

He pulls me to my feet and forces me up the ladder. Heath is already at the top, ready to pull me along with Alec at his side. Jamison and Mak follow. My legs feel like they are going to continuously give out. We are close to the tracks when a Free World SUV pulls in front of us. My brother's and Maksim swear and start to back track, but when the window rolls down, a familiar voice calls to us.

"Come on!" Ivan Brookes yells. There is a woman in the passenger seat who I don't know, but I trust Ivan. I remember his face when they took me.

"Brookes?" I gasp through tears.

"There isn't much time! Let's go!"

My legs carry me on my own to the SUV. I get in the third row with Maksim and Heath. Jamison and Alec get in the second row and Ivan pulls onto the rocky road, headed south.

The only sound for a while is the sound of our breathing. My body trembles and words escape me. How did I let us leave them behind? My own mother. Maksim had a chance at being with his mother again, but he left to protect me. I know I should be grateful, but there is something boiling inside. I hug my knees against my chest and bite the inside of my cheek. I feel Maksim's eyes occasionally but refuse to look back at him.

"How did you find us, Ivan?" Jamison asks.

"I saw you guys run from our apartment and told Ivan," the woman says. "He said he knew you and we just had to help."

"And who are you?" Maksim questions.

"His wife, Adella," she smiles back at us. I look at Ivan in the mirror.

He smiles softly at me. "I'm sorry I couldn't help you before, Wren. I didn't know that was going to happen," he says.

"I know … thank you for coming," I reply. I don't even try to fake a smile.

Jamison starts giving Ivan directions to the southern coast. I look down at my moms' jacket. It smells like her and makes more tears fill my eyes. If her and Katherine would have just come with us, we could have outrun the New World Order. We could have made it somewhere safe. Maksim looks over at me and nudges me gently. I force myself to look at him.

"I'm so … so sorry," he whispers. My throat clenches and I feel fresh tears run down my cheeks. "I wanted to get everyone out. I thought we could do it," he shakes his head.

"When did you agree to leave her behind if necessary?" I hiss.

"Last night," he answers. "Wren, she begged me. I was going to be the one to stay behind. She fought me. She wasn't taking no for an answer. She asked one thing of me," he rambles. I sit and clench my jaw, waiting. "She only asked that I protect you and get you away from the New World Order … to give you a normal life."

"Wren …" Heath sighs. "I heard her. I saw her fight with him. She had her own agenda," he tells me firmly. "She's our mother … and mother's make sacrifices."

"She didn't have to. We could have made it."

"And they would have caught on and found us or tracked us and we would be stuck in this never-ending cycle of rescuing each other and losing each other!" he snaps. I look down and smother a sob from my throat.

"It should have been me …" I cry.

"Wren … I know this hurts, but please. Please, accept this. Let it go. Move on. You have to heal physically and mentally," Alec turns around and grabs my hands. I see the tears in his eyes too. I look back at Maksim, who is now staring out his window.

"I know you're hurt," he mutters. I close my eyes tight and cover my face with my hands. "I feel … like a part of me has been ripped out … seeing my mom and losing her all over again," he chokes.

"She loves you, Maksim," I tell him.

"And that's what sucks, doesn't it?" he growls. I can't bring myself to reply. There is nothing I can say or do that is going to change anything that has happened.

We drive for the entire day. I keep myself from shaking by hugging my knees to my chest and keeping my head down. Late evening, the car stops, and I look up to see the familiar beach huts. We all get out of the car and stretch for a little while, saying nothing. I notice something about Adella ... her belly has a bump. Her body is petite and when she turns to the side, a perfectly rounded bump rests on her hips. Brookes sees me staring and smiles again.

"I couldn't start a family in that place. Not after what Isabelle did to you," he whispers to me.

I nod and smile at Adella. "Protecting your family first ... you're not who I thought you were," I mumble and walk towards the water.

I stand alone for a long time, watching the waves crash against each other. As I expected, Maksim joins me. I hug myself against the breeze and keep my eyes down. He holds a bag over to me. I glance at his hand and take it.

"I grabbed some of your clothes," he says in a flat tone.

"Thank you ... for thinking of that."

Silence. Painful silence.

"I wish ... I wish I could have convinced your mom to let it be me," he blurts out.

"I would have fought for you too," I counter.

"So, don't you see?" he demands, turning to me. "There was no winning. Between your mother and I ... someone was going to be left behind for one reason or another. She chose and there was no fighting her," he tells me. "As much as it kills me ... knowing how hurt you are and feeling the pain of losing my own mother all over again ... I still have purpose and reason to keep going and move on with time," his voice turns icy again, like I am so familiar with. "I have you," he motions to me.

"We all could have made –"

"No," he cuts me off. "Not without repeating this cycle."

"I will get revenge," I snap.

"No. I'm not letting you go back there."

"Have you not been paying attention?" I hiss. "No one can tell me what I can or can't do."

"Please. Please stop this," he begs.

"What do you want from me?" I whimper.

"Let it all go. At least for a little while. I'm angry too … but seven people, one being pregnant, are no match against the New World Order. We need to find real support … and that means leaving here."

"Where will we go?"

"West. Far west. But we can't do that if you keep running off to get revenge. I want it too. I want it so bad. Not just for those we have lost … but for *you*," he reaches out and touches my shoulder hesitantly. I think for a long time.

"Make me a promise," I look at him in the eye.

"Anything."

"No more splitting up. No more going off and doing our own thing. We work better together. No secrets, no lies and no decisions made without talking to one another. We can leave. We can find real help. And when we do … I want the New World Order *and* the Free World destroyed," I tell him.

His hand drops to his side and he looks back at the others as they unpack things into two huts. He looks at the waves and the sky. Everywhere but me.

"It won't be easy," he sighs. "But … I promise, I will do everything I can to make that happen." He agrees, looking down at me. I hold out my hand and he smiles slightly, shaking it with his.

"We are completely, one hundred percent on the same side, okay?" I grip his hand tight.

"I've been on your side for a long time," he grins. I look at the others and start walking towards the huts.

"What's our next move?" I ask.

He stops me and makes me face him again. "You rest … and be patient. Give us time to figure out a plan that will get us what we want," he answers, looking back at my brother's as they unload the car.

Patience has never been my friend. I know how this game will go. They are going to do everything they can to keep me away from the New World Order. If anything is going to get done … I'm going to have to do it alone.

CHAPTER 21

Two Months Later

We left thc coast because it's what was best for us. I wanted to put as much distance between us and the New World Order as possible before Adella had her baby. We ended up further South and West. Jamison wanted to keep going until we hit the water, but it was getting to be too much for Adella. He wanted to make Wren happy. She was happy on the coast. She loved the ocean. The few days before her mother's execution, she would actually smile. Genuinely. Every morning, I would watch her walk down to the water without shoes and with her jeans rolled up. She started collecting shells, lining them up on her windowsill in her bedroom. After the execution, we left. Wren was heartbroken because of losing her mother and to top it off, we were leaving the place she loved.

I was losing hope right before the Everett girls found us. We were completely lost when they came along in an old red pickup. They were on their way home from church. They took us in. The Everett's live in a big plantation home that was untouched during the Third War. They went to a church a few miles away from their home with a few other Independents. They don't belong to any Territory. There is no ruling government down here, so for us, this place was perfect. Doris Everett and her daughters were kind enough to open their home for as long as we needed.

Shortly after getting settled in with them, Adella had a baby girl. Ember. The day she was born was the most I had ever seen Wren smile. Even when we were at the coast, nothing topped this. Ember was proof there was still some good that could come from the world. She became a light at the end of a very long, dark tunnel for all of us. I knew it couldn't last forever, but I wanted it to last just a little longer. Long enough for Wren to grieve and move on. I'm starting to see that there may not be enough time in the world for her to really heal.

"We need to get her away from here," Heath growls. Jamison and I exchange doubtful looks. "She's gotten obsessed with revenge. You two like to ignore the warning signs, but Alec and I refuse."

"We aren't ignoring the warning signs, Heath," Jamison sighs. "We are giving her space."

"You said you would protect her. You promised," Alec snaps at me. I glare over at him and bite my tongue. "Nothing to say? Do you not see what is happening to her? She's falling apart!"

"I can't stop that," I hiss. "She is alive and unharmed. I've kept my promise."

"What about her mental and emotional wellness?" Heath questions.

I can't help but laugh. "I am the *last* person that should try to help her with that," I scoff. Before I can argue anymore, Ivan comes barreling into the room looking pale.

"Where's Wren?" he demands.

"What do you mean? She's in her room." Heath answers him.

"No, she's not. Adella and I checked. She's nowhere upstairs and I can't find her down here either," he shakes his head.

All four of us are on our feet in a second. Doris and her daughters even start looking. Doris goes outside and a few minutes later, comes back in looking concerned.

"What is it?" Jamison asks.

"The truck is gone. The guns are gone," she tells us.

"She left. She's going to do this alone," I close my eyes tight and try to slow my breathing.

"It's okay, Maksim," Jamison grabs my shoulder. "We'll get to her. We just need to figure out how," he sighs.

"We don't know how long ago she left, Jamison. She could be too far ahead for us to catch up."

"So, we don't catch up and just find her there before she does anything reckless," Alec grumbles. I want to punch something. Anything. I've never met anyone so infuriating in my life.

"She *is* reckless!" I snap. "She's a ticking time bomb!"

"Calm down. We need to think," Heath growls. *She agreed to be patient. She lied.*

"There is a train that passes through here sometimes. If you can catch it going in the right direction, it will take you as far East as you can go," Doris tells us.

"It can get us back to the coast," Jamison nods. "And from there, we can go North."

"She may not even be alive by the time we get there," I spit.

"Don't say that," Heath rolls his eyes. "She's not as fragile as you like to make her seem. She'll be fine. She'll go somewhere safe and start planning. That gives us time."

"I know she's not fragile, but she is a walking target! What makes you think she'll take time to plan? We agree she's not thinking clearly, don't we?" I demand.

"I know her, Maksim. She won't do anything without a plan. She probably had this little escape planned out for weeks. Give her some credit," he rubs his eyes. I look to Jamison for help.

"We need to get to her and finish this once and for all, before they find her and kill her," I shake my head.

He grabs my shoulders and looks me in the eye. "We are going to get to her, Soldier. I promise. She's going to be okay until then. I'm afraid you've only known her at some of her weakest moments. She's strong and she's smart."

"I know," I try to shrug him away. He shakes me back into focus.

"We go get her and we do just like you said. We finish this. And then there's no more running away. No more keeping her under lock and key. We'll all be free," he smiles. I nod and step out of reach.

I have a promise to keep. Elissa Adler begged me to take care of Wren. Give her a normal life even. She believed I was capable of doing that. I want her to be right. I have to get to Wren, and I have to help her finish this. I can't expect her to stay on the sidelines. As much as I hate it ... I have to let her take the lead and whatever fights come her way, I have to be beside her, fighting those fights. Not *for* her, but *with* her.

So … if you're reading this, I guess that means there is hope. But we aren't done yet. Frankly, we've barely begun. I didn't know it at the time, but I was going to realize that I hadn't seen anything yet. The rebellion and the battles … they were nothing compared to what was to come. The pain and the loss that we have all endured is just the beginning.

ABOUT THE AUTHOR

Caitlyn Gilmore is entering her sophomore year as a Music Education major. She plays multiple instruments but specializes in clarinet, violin, cello and piano. Caitlyn has composed original music as well as arranged pieces for small chamber ensembles and string quartets. Aside for her love for music and teaching she possesses a lifelong love reading and writing. Caitlyn developed a passion for reading fiction novels during early childhood. As she approached her teenage years, she began to flex her creative writing muscles by submitting short stories to various writing competitions. Throughout her high school career, she received impressive feedback from a number of educators that her creative writing should be shared with others. This positive encouragement led her to write and publish this particular book.

Printed in the United States
By Bookmasters